"What we shared," Zach continued, "was something—"

"Something?" Claire cried, almost dissolving into tears. It had been *everything!* Because she had saved herself for this man. And why? Because she was in love with him, damn it!

"Special," he said.

"No," she said. "Sex is meaningless if all it amounts to is two bodies clinging together for a brief time, then turning away from each other indifferently."

"Don't belittle yourself or me like that!" he begged.

But his remorse had come too little and too late. The damage has been done. "You only say that because you feel guilty."

"Yes."

"Well you're not alone in your misery—let's please forget what happened between us."

D0012606

CATHERINE SPENCER, once an English teacher, fell into writing through eavesdropping on a conversation about Harlequin romances. Within two months she changed careers and sold her first book to Harlequin in 1984. She moved to Canada from England thirty years ago and lives in Vancouver. She is married to a Canadian and has four grown children—two daughters and two sons—plus three dogs and a cat. In her spare time she plays the piano, collects antiques and grows tropical shrubs.

Books by Catherine Spencer

HARLEQUIN PRESENTS®

1873—DOMINIC'S CHILD
1927—CHRISTMAS WITH A STRANGER
1950—A NANNY IN THE FAMILY
1976—TEMPTING LUCAS
2016—DANTE'S TWINS
2101—THE UNEXPECTED WEDDING GIFT

Don't miss any of our special offers. Write to us at the following address for information on our newest releases.

Harlequin Reader Service
U.S.: 3010 Walden Ave., P.O. Box 1325, Buffalo, NY 14269
Canadian: P.O. Box 609, Fort Erie, Ont. L2A 5X3

Catherine Spencer

ZACHARY'S VIRGIN

HARLEQUIN®

TORONTO • NEW YORK • LONDON
AMSTERDAM • PARIS • SYDNEY • HAMBURG
STOCKHOLM • ATHENS • TOKYO • MILAN • MADRID
PRAGUE • WARSAW • BUDAPEST • AUCKLAND

If you purchased this book without a cover you should be aware
that this book is stolen property. It was reported as "unsold and
destroyed" to the publisher, and neither the author nor the
publisher has received any payment for this "stripped book."

ISBN 0-373-12143-1

ZACHARY'S VIRGIN

First North American Publication 2000.

Copyright © 1999 by Kathy Garner.

All rights reserved. Except for use in any review, the reproduction or
utilization of this work in whole or in part in any form by any electronic,
mechanical or other means, now known or hereafter invented, including
xerography, photocopying and recording, or in any information storage
or retrieval system, is forbidden without the written permission of the
publisher, Harlequin Enterprises Limited, 225 Duncan Mill Road,
Don Mills, Ontario, Canada M3B 3K9.

All characters in this book have no existence outside the imagination of
the author and have no relation whatsoever to anyone bearing the same
name or names. They are not even distantly inspired by any individual
known or unknown to the author, and all incidents are pure invention.

This edition published by arrangement with Harlequin Books S.A.

® and TM are trademarks of the publisher. Trademarks indicated with
® are registered in the United States Patent and Trademark Office, the
Canadian Trade Marks Office and in other countries.

Visit us at www.eHarlequin.com

Printed in U.S.A.

CHAPTER ONE

THE brochures made the Topaz Valley Ski Resort sound like paradise. Deep in the mountains of British Columbia, Canada's most westerly province, it appeared to possess all the winter sports advantages of St. Moritz, with the added bonus of being reasonably close to Vancouver, the city where Claire hoped to open another in her chain of successful jewelry boutiques. That it was far removed from her usual haunts and circle of friends remained yet another point in its favor because the fact was, she needed a change of scene.

Amazing, she had to admit, that she, who had worked so long and hard to inch her way to the top of Europe's society heap, should know a sudden longing to make contact with a simpler, more basic way of life. But lately, when she looked in the mirror, she had seen a stranger looking back at her, one so concerned with keeping up appearances that she had neglected to nurture the private, fragile part of herself no one else knew. Too much more of that and she was afraid that other person, the *real* Claire Durocher, would disappear forever.

Topaz Valley had seemed to offer the chance she was seeking to take stock, not just of how far she'd come since she'd left behind the squalid life she'd known as a child in Marseilles but, more important, where she was headed next. But the brochures which had made the resort sound so attractive had neglected to state that British Columbia was vast and untamed. Or that, once she arrived in Canada, it would take the better part of another six hours to reach her destination and that, toward the end of her journey, she would be so weary that she would have paid a small ransom to lie down on a soft bed and sleep undisturbed for a further twelve hours.

And not once had it mentioned that, while the narrow strip of coast around Vancouver enjoyed mild green winters, with late roses still blooming in sheltered gardens, the interior of the province lay in the death grip of a cold which no outsider could begin to comprehend until she experienced it firsthand.

Of course, she had expected snow, and from the little she could see when she stepped down from the helicopter at her journey's end, there was plenty of it. But it was the wind which dismayed her. It cut clean through to the bone, and left her gasping for breath.

Her seven other fellow passengers seemed unaffected by the subarctic conditions. Indeed, they were astonishingly cheerful. Huddled in their bulky jackets, they turned their backs to the wind and, as a pair of headlights speared the afternoon gloom and crawled up the hill toward them, began a jolly rendition of "Here Comes Santa Claus."

Claire had to admire their fortitude. For her part, she was beginning to wonder if Christmas in Canada had been such a good idea after all, particularly when, having stashed the last of the luggage and equipment against a wooden rack erected for the purpose, the pilot waved to his passengers, called out, "Merry Christmas, folks! I'm off while the going's still good," and climbed back inside his helicopter with what struck her as ominous haste.

In seconds, the rotors picked up speed and with the clumsy grace of some prehistoric bird, the craft lifted off, severing her last link with civilization as she knew it. "What on earth possessed me to think this would be a novel way to spend the holidays?" she muttered, clutching her fur-trimmed hood beneath her chin and staring at the bleak landscape surrounding her.

Already the sky to the east had taken on the purplish hue of approaching night while that to the west showed the sort of pewter overcast which heralded more snow. And the wind...!

The vehicle to which the headlights were attached crested the slope of the hill and groaned to a halt. A burly figure muffled to the eyebrows in clothes designed to withstand an assault on Everest hefted his bulk out of the driver's seat and lifted one padded arm in cheery welcome.

"Here we are, folks! Topaz Valley's limo at your service, heh, heh, heh! Climb aboard all those who don't feel up to hiking down to the lodge."

His attempt at humor might have lacked the sophistication she was used to, but Claire had to admit he showed singular gallantry in the speed with which he hoisted her up inside the...what was it? Square as a box, it resembled an army tank from the outside—if one discounted the bright yellow paint, that was—but inside were three rows of stark wooden seats, ample room for suitcases and skis and, praise heaven, warmth blasting over one's ankles from a heater. For this last, she forgave the vehicle its other shortcomings.

"You're lucky you got here," the driver announced, slamming closed the door and settling himself behind the steering wheel. "Yesterday's party got held up overnight in Broome, visibility was so bad up here. Had to bunk down in the Wayside Motel and make do with hamburgers at the truck stop, which is a far cry from what they'd been expecting for dinner, I can tell you."

Feeling increasingly estranged from everything familiar, Claire peered out of the window as the vehicle jolted along a path between snow-laden trees, across a plateau and around a curve, with no sign of civilization to relieve the windswept landscape. But then, just when she'd about given up hope of ever laying eyes on the resort, suddenly there it lay, in a hollow protecting it from the worst of the weather, and she drew in a breath of relief. Windows ablaze with golden light and smoke streaming from its chimneys, the place exuded warmth.

Flinging open the vehicle doors, the driver clambered out onto hard-packed snow. "Watch your step as you get down, folks. We've sanded twice today already, but it's still a mite icy underfoot."

Indeed it was, and the temperature surely dipping well below what she was used to, but a man had come out of the lodge to welcome them. Engagingly handsome, with sun-bleached hair, an open smile, and the slim, fit body of a professional athlete, he couldn't possibly be the legendary owner of the place, Claire decided. He was much too young to have achieved such success.

"Glad you made it before we got socked in by the weather again," he said. "Come on inside and warm up, before you all freeze."

Not the most socially acceptable greeting, perhaps, but possessed of undeniable charm nonetheless. Much like the building, Claire supposed, glancing up at the impressive facade. Neither the fairy-tale nineteenth-century castles nor quaint chalets she was used to, it stood bold and dramatically beautiful in its own right, with soaring timbers, chimneys faced with chunks of river rock worn smooth by centuries of water abrasion, and great shining expanses of glass.

Designed around a central hub from which four wings radiated, it rose three stories to a steeply pitched roof. Entering through wide double doors, Claire gazed around, her senses assaulted by impressions of spacious elegance and mammoth proportions. Everything, from the graceful branched staircase accessing the upper galleries, to the massive beams supporting the vaulted ceiling, to the stone fireplace whose hearth was wide enough to accommodate a grown man, was huge.

Even the Christmas tree stood some twenty feet high and was hung with silver balls the size of fat balloons. As for the leather couches grouped around the hearth, they could have accommodated giants and still left room for normal-size people.

And everywhere, from the long refectory table in the middle of the room, to the deep windowsills, to the antique wicker child's sleigh beside the fireplace, the brilliant splash of carmine poinsettias drew the eye. If that weren't enough to complete the Christmas card picture, two beautiful Samoyeds lay on a rug in front of the fire, basking in the heat from the blazing logs.

Joining the lineup of guests checking in, Claire studied the floor plan of the lodge hanging on the wall behind the front desk. Whoever had designed the resort had certainly taken pains to make sure guests were supplied with every possible amenity. In addition to various lounges, a library, and dining room, there was also a banquet room with a dance floor, a movie theater, gymnasium, sauna, indoor pool, and a beauty spa offering everything from facials and manicures to massages. And oh, she could use a soothing massage just then, to ease the aching stiffness caused by so many hours spent in travel!

The couple at the front desk, their check-in complete, moved away and made room for Claire.

"Hi!" The clerk, a young woman whose name tag proclaimed her to be Sally, smiled warmly and scanned the list of names in front of her. "Let's see, you must be...?"

"Claire Durocher."

"Oh, sure! All the way from Europe, right? Welcome to

Canada!'' She glanced again at the list. "Originally, we had you booked into a suite here in the main lodge.''

"Indeed, yes,'' Claire said, not liking the sound of the word "originally.'' She had slept fitfully on the transatlantic flight, her inner clock was seriously out of kilter, and she hadn't bathed since she left Paris yesterday afternoon. To find now that she had no room at the inn didn't bear thinking about. "Such accommodation was what I requested when I made my reservation six months ago, it was confirmed by your office within the week as I'm sure your records show, and it is what I now expect to receive.''

The young clerk's grin faded a little. "Yeah…well, the thing is, we've had to put you in one of our other rooms. It's rather small but very comfortable and it's only for a night or two.''

"I do not wish to be confined to a smaller room, nor do I wish to move elsewhere when you decide it is convenient. I wish to be accommodated in the suite I reserved.''

"I'm afraid that's not possible,'' the Sally person said. "The people occupying it last week haven't left yet.''

"Then put *them* in the smaller room,'' Claire replied, ignoring the little voice inside her that said it was easier simply to accept whatever was available and not make a fuss. She had learned the hard way that if she wanted others to treat her with the respect she craved and which had been so sadly lacking in her childhood, she had to demand the best of—and for—herself.

The hapless Sally shook her head. "You don't understand, Miss Durocher. They won't fit. They're a family of four.''

"Zut!" Claire exclaimed, her tone rising with annoyance.

"Is there a problem?'' By comparison, the voice which

flowed over her shoulder was smooth and rich as the finest Belgian chocolate.

"Oh, Zach!" The young clerk fairly wilted with relief. "It's the business with the Dogwood Suite. Miss Durocher is a little upset that it's not available."

"Miss Durocher is more than a little upset," Claire corrected, swinging round to confront the man whose name tag identified him as Zachary Alexander, the owner of the establishment and the person with whom she'd made her reservations. "She is considerably...displeased...."

He stood well over six feet, every lean muscle honed to perfection, the torso tapering gracefully from impressively broad shoulders to narrow hips, the hair thick and dark except for streaks of silver at the temples.

As for the face—oh, it was the face that left her stumbling over her words like an ingenue. Such eyes, as blue as the Bay of Naples in summer and as remote as the tips of the Alps on a perfect winter day. Such a jaw, such cheekbones! And the mouth...!

Her own ran dry at the sight. Zachary Alexander could discipline that mouth all he liked. Make it straight and severe, or allow it to stretch in a tight, unamused smile as he inspected his unhappy guest. But nothing his will imposed could erase the passionate nature betrayed by the curve of the upper lip. This was a sleeping volcano of a man, his fire hidden but no less intense for all that.

"I'm sure we're all very sorry that you're..." Again, that ironic smile touched his mouth. "...considerably displeased, but the fact remains that the suite you requested is occupied already so I'm afraid you have no choice but to accept the substitute we're offering—unless, of course, you'd prefer to sleep outside in the snow?"

You can't be tired just yet and what child wants to go to bed early on such a warm night? Go wait in the street,

*Claire, and leave Mama to entertain her gentleman friend
in peace, and if you're very good, maybe there'll be enough
money for a bonbon tomorrow....*

Her mother's voice floated down the years, finding the
chink in her armor so susceptible to a brush-off and spur-
ring Claire to take issue with Zachary Alexander's assump-
tion that she'd meekly make do with whatever consolation
prize he chose to throw in her direction. Impaling him in
her most peremptory stare, she said, "I have been en route
to Topaz Valley for almost twenty-four hours, *monsieur,* of
which six have been spent making connecting flights from
Vancouver. I could have flown from my home in
Switzerland or my pied à terre in France, to any of the
capitals in Europe in less time than it has taken to complete
this last limb of my journey and I—"

"Considering that this province alone is approximately
twenty-three times the size of your country, that's hardly
surprising." The reply was polite enough—if one were to
discount the fact that he cut her off in mid-sentence, in the
sort of patronizing tone that suggested he was dealing with
a singularly difficult and backward child. "Add to that the
fact that, whereas the population of Switzerland runs to
some four hundred and four people per square mile, there
are a mere eight point two per square mile in British
Columbia, and it—"

"And it is my misfortune to have to do business with
the point two—a man of few brains and absolutely no
heart!" At the twitch of yet another smile which he barely
managed to contain, Claire stamped one booted foot im-
periously. "I am tired, I am hungry, I would like to unpack
my suitcases, take a long, undisturbed, hot bath, and I am
in no mood to tolerate being laughed at or inconvenienced,
Monsieur Alexander!"

"And I am in no mood to tolerate your self-indulgent

tantrums, Mademoiselle Durocher, so I suggest you lower your voice and modify your attitude. Your suite is not available and that's all there is to it. The family who should have vacated it yesterday have a sick child who is not fit to travel and until he is recovered, I have no intention of asking them to find some other place to stay.''

It had been years since Claire had blushed but his announcement left her face burning. "I am so sorry," she began, at once remorseful and embarrassed. "Had you explained, I would, of course, have understood.''

"You scarcely gave me the chance," Zachary Alexander said curtly and turned again to his desk clerk. "What else have we got besides the room on the second floor?''

"Nothing in the main lodge, which is where Ms. Durocher asked to stay.''

"What about the lakeside guest houses?''

"Nothing there, either. The only thing not taken is the private suite at your place, Zach, but Eric usually stays there over the holidays.''

"Well, since he's neither shown up as expected nor bothered to let me know what his plans are, he's out of luck this year. As of now, the place is occupied by Ms. Durocher. If he puts in an appearance, he'll have to make do with the room she finds so unacceptable." Zachary Alexander didn't so much turn his head to look at Claire as glance obliquely at her, in the way that a man might if he wished to avoid antagonizing a rabid poodle. "Get Paul to haul her stuff over, once he's free, and I'll get her settled.''

Picking up her overnight bag, he led Claire to the back of the foyer and through another set of double doors to the outside. Dusk had fallen but lights, strung from one snow-encrusted evergreen to the next like outsize charms on a giant bracelet, showed a path winding among the trees to a series of guest houses nestled along the lakeshore. Scaled-down versions of the main lodge, they were substantial, charming residences and looked nothing like the rustic cabins Claire had envisioned.

"We're down this way," he said, turning right at a fork in the path.

A few minutes later, his house came into view. Set apart from the rest and screened by a belt of dark-needled conifers, it was different, larger, and even grander than its neighbors. Shaped like the letter T and fronted on all sides by a long, covered veranda, it hugged a cozy hollow on a spit of land just a few yards short of the lake itself. Again, Claire was pleasantly surprised. She had not expected quite such elegance in the hinterland.

"We live in this end of the house," her reluctant host announced, indicating the upper two-thirds of the letter T, "but you've got the rest of the building all to yourself."

She followed him up a shallow flight of steps to one of the verandas and waited as he unlocked a door to the left. Reaching inside, he turned on the lights, dropped the key in the palm of her hand, and said, "I'm afraid you'll find only one outsize living room with breakfast bar and convenience kitchenette, one large bedroom, a dressing room and a five-piece bathroom with attached sauna. I sincerely hope you won't be too cramped for space."

Having delivered that salvo, he then dumped her overnight bag on the threshold and turned to go.

"One moment, monsieur, if you please," she said, wishing she sounded less coldly formal. Her thoughts, her inner voice, were fluent and colloquial but when it came to translating them from French to English, especially when she was nervous or under stress, she knew her spoken words lacked eloquence and often sounded stilted and unfriendly.

"Yes?"

"I am not the unreasonable woman you perceive me to be," she said, touching him placatingly on the arm, "and if I seemed that way, I apologize. When a child is taken ill, of course one must be prepared to make allowances."

He looked at where her hand rested on the sleeve of his sweater, then lifted his gaze to her face. His eyes were cold as ice, his voice not much warmer. "Enjoy your stay, Ms. Durocher, and do let us know if there's anything more we can do to cater to your comfort."

Speechless, she watched as he marched away, stunned by such controlled displeasure, such proud disdain. What a pity a man so tall and beautiful was possessed of such an untoward nature!

Another party of guests had arrived by road when he got back to the main lodge. They swarmed around the lobby, but Sally had roped in extra help at the desk and seemed to be coping, so he skirted the crowd and made his way down the south wing to the kitchen.

There'd been no sign of life at the house, which meant either that Mel hadn't come down the hill yet or else she was cadging food from Roberto the chef. It had better, he thought dourly, be the latter. The lifts would be closing in ten minutes and he was in no mood to go searching for an errant thirteen-year-old who'd suddenly decided she didn't have to abide by the rules which governed other people.

Pushing aside the swing doors, he poked his head inside the kitchen. Various pots simmered on the huge stainless steel stove. Baguettes, freshly baked in the special bread oven he'd had imported from France, cooled on wire racks on the marble counter. The young kid hired for the season to help out with food preparation was busy slicing tomatoes. At the far end of the room, Roberto consulted with

Simon, the wine steward. Of Mel, however, there was no sign.

"Anyone seen my daughter?" Zach inquired.

"She was here about ten minutes ago," Roberto said. "And starving, as usual."

Zach nodded. It never ceased to amaze him how much food Mel could put away and still remain skinny as a reed. "I'll leave you to it, then. We've got a full house tonight so if you need extra help, let me know."

Back in the lobby, the crowd had thinned. His wrangler and man Friday, McBride, the person he trusted most in the world, was dumping a fresh load of logs in the big brass box next to the hearth. "If I didn't know better," he said, thumbing back his Stetson and regarding Zach from beneath bushy gray brows, "I'd say you look like a man with a load of woman troubles."

"You're not far off the mark," he said gloomily. "A jet-setting heiress with a bad case of perma-pout arrived this afternoon and it's my guess we'll be seeing and hearing a lot more of her than any of us would like before Christmas is over."

"Heiress, you say? She here alone?"

"Yes."

"Ugly?"

An image flashed across Zach's mind, of huge gray eyes and silky black lashes in a delicate heart-shaped face; of a cupid's bow mouth and small, perfect teeth. Of fine-boned hands and a fall of dark hair; of slender shoulders raised in protest and a narrow, elegant foot stamping in annoyance. Pity she had the temperament of a pit viper!

He gave a noncommittal shrug. "I've seen worse."

McBride looked hopeful. "Yeah? She lookin' for a husband by any chance?"

"There's no doubt you're a fine figure of a man and able

to sweep just about any woman off her feet," Zach said, grinning, "but this one's young enough to be your daughter."

"Well, shee-oot!" The old wrangler cackled. "Can't blame a guy for askin'. Maybe you're the one should be setting his sights on her."

Zach sobered. "When hell freezes over!"

McBride crooked one corner of his mouth and gnawed on his mustache a moment. "At thirty-eight, you're awful young yourself, Zach, to be so set in your ways. Jenny's been dead goin' on six years and that little gal of yours needs a mama, else she'll be growing up wild as a cayuse. Already she can cuss better'n me and that's sayin' plenty. Jenny wouldn't like that, son, and you and I both know it. If she'd lived, she'd have seen to it that Melanie learned her party manners and wore a skirt once in a while, instead of always hangin' around the joint in blue jeans and your cast-off sweaters."

But Jenny hadn't lived, and although the shock of losing her so suddenly and senselessly had faded, Zach couldn't imagine anyone else ever filling her place, least of all someone like the Durocher woman. Jenny had been soft and sweet and patient; able to turn her hand to whatever needed doing, whether it was teaching beginners on the ski hill, lending a hand at the front desk, or helping in the kitchen. And in between, she'd been a devoted wife and a wonderful mother.

"Mel's got plenty of time before she needs to worry about dressing up for parties," he declared, and wished he felt as sure as he sounded. A year ago, he'd never have questioned his ability to handle his daughter. She'd been content with the kind of life he provided and seemed to love the isolation that came with it.

He'd set her up with her own computer, enrolled her in

correspondence school, worked with her on her class assignments. He'd taught her to ski, to skate, to swim. McBride had taught her to ride and shoot a mean game of pool. Her days had been full and exciting and she hadn't seemed to miss friends her own age.

But over the summer, something had changed. She'd begun harping on about going away to school. She didn't seem as eager to spend leisure time with him anymore. They hadn't skied together once this season. Either she had her nose buried in a magazine or else she went off by herself. Sometimes, he'd find her in whispered conversation with Sally, but the moment she saw him approaching, she'd close up tighter than a clam.

He'd always known there'd come a time when she'd want to talk to a woman about...womanly things. But he hadn't bargained on it happening this soon.

"She's only thirteen, for crying out loud."

"In case you didn't know, son, that's about the time when all hell breaks loose." With the tip of his tongue, McBride probed experimentally at one of his molars. "From what I've heard tell, the teenage years ain't ever easy. Even with two parents, it's a full-time job keepin' on top of things."

People were drifting downstairs and coming in from the guest houses for happy hour. Craning his neck, Zach could see across the lobby to the lounge where the staff was setting out a selection of hot and cold hors d'oeuvres. Charlie and Walter were already manning the bar.

"Well, I'm damned if I'm going wife hunting just to give Mel two parents," he told McBride, "so she's just going to have to make do with one. I'm off to change before dinner. If you happen to see her, tell her to make tracks for home ASAP."

The wind had dropped when he went outside and it had

started to snow, tiny sparkling flakes that signaled another dip in the temperature. Seasonal music floated out softly from the speakers mounted under the eaves. The thousand or more lights strung along the roofline and over the veranda railings of the lodge flung a blanket of light over the frozen, snow-packed ground. The pungent smell of wood smoke hung in the air.

He inhaled a long, relaxing breath. The skies were forecast to have cleared by tomorrow, it was December the eighteenth, and in three days the holiday program would be underway, beginning with the traditional moonlight sleigh ride. He had better things to concentrate on than one nitpicking guest.

Hunching his jacket collar more snugly around his neck, he set out along the path to the house, the conversation with McBride playing over again in his mind. Was he wrong in thinking he could be both mother and father to Mel? Did she miss Jenny more than either of them realized?

The Samoyeds bounded ahead with Blanche nipping playfully at Lily's heels as usual in a race to arrive home first. Turning the last corner, he saw with some relief that the lights in his section of the house were on, which meant that Melanie was already there. Too bad the remaining third was also lit up brighter than a Christmas tree. If he had to be saddled with someone next door, he could think of a dozen people he'd rather play host to than Claire Durocher. Even Eric, his flake of a brother-in-law, was preferable to her.

Music blasted into the night, something festively bright and boisterous, punctuated by gales of laughter. Oh, yeah, his daughter was home, all right! Better warn her to keep the noise down for the next few days, unless she wanted to run afoul of their neighbor.

He stamped the snow from his boots and opened the

front door, expecting to find Melanie sprawled out in front of the TV. But the family room at the far end of the entrance hall was empty.

Only then did he realize the music was coming from next door and so was the laughter, the woman's rich as hot buttered rum and the girl's—his daughter's—high and gleeful.

Damn! He'd seen more than enough of his petulant European guest for one day, but it looked as if he wasn't through with her quite yet. Because just lately, Melanie had attitude to spare and the last thing she needed was further instruction from a willful, self-indulgent woman like Claire Durocher.

Heaving a sigh of pure exasperation, he slammed shut his own front door and marched purposefully toward his neighbor's.

CHAPTER TWO

IN MANY ways, the girl reminded her of herself as she'd been at the same age; a little urchin whose brave, tough exterior hid a heart as uncertain and vulnerable as that of a newborn lamb.

"Oh, heck," she'd said, her face falling in dismay when Claire had opened the door to her knock. "You're not Eric."

"Well, no. At least, I wasn't the last time I looked in the mirror."

Claire had laughed, but the girl, obviously not expecting to be welcomed by a stranger, had turned away, her shoulders slumped dejectedly. "Sorry I bugged you by banging on the door then."

"*Chérie*, please wait. I don't know anyone here and you're my first visitor."

"I'm not supposed to bother the guests."

"But you're not bothering me." She'd held out her hand. "Here, let's introduce ourselves and make our association official. I'm Claire Durocher."

The child had turned bright red and offered a not-too-clean little paw. "Melanie," she'd mumbled and, at Claire's urging, stepped inside the suite.

Claire had learned early to build a nest wherever she happened to find herself, be it a shop doorway or a château, and Topaz Valley Resort was no exception. No sooner had she hung her clothes in the dressing room closet and set out her toiletries in the adjoining bathroom than she'd turned her attention to the salon. Already, candles burned on the low table before the double-sided fireplace which opened into the bedroom also.

She had closed the dark red drapes to shut out the bleak afternoon, tossed another log on the fire, and flung her royal blue mohair shawl over one arm of the soft leather couch. Not that the place lacked comfort—indeed, it was luxuriously appointed, right down to the fresh fruit and flowers—but a few personal touches made it seem more of a home.

Still, Melanie clearly felt anything but comfortable. Fiddling all the while with the hem of her oversize sweater, she peered around furtively as if she expected that, at any moment, she'd be shown the door.

It had been more than sixteen years since Claire had experienced much the same fear, never sure if she was welcome in the two rooms which had been home, or if she should make herself scarce in the back alley until such time as yet another of her mother's "gentleman friends" left, but the memories had not faded with time. She doubted they ever would; the sense of abandonment had left too deep a scar. Observing her uncertain little guest sympathetically, she said, "Why don't you find us some music while I make up a little plate of hors d'oeuvres? Choose something you enjoy, *ma chère*—something lively and fun."

"Okay."

Melanie leaped at the chance to make herself useful while Claire set to work. The kitchenette Zachary Alexander had spoken of contained a wine bar with a refrigerator, a microwave oven, cappuccino coffeemaker and small sink. Various wineglasses and tall mugs hung from a rack, and a cupboard next to the refrigerator contained a supply of flavored coffees, hot chocolate, nuts and other snacks.

"It's too early for *champagne*," she said, checking the contents of the refrigerator, "but we can enjoy a cranberry cocktail while we get to know one another, yes?"

Melanie looked up from the compact discs she was sorting and giggled. "You talk funny," she said. "Nobody here says 'shompanya,' they just call it plain old champagne."

"Well, I'm French so I say some things a little differently, but I'm going to count on you to tell me if I make mistakes." As she talked, Claire poured sparkling cranberry juice into two crystal goblets, set them on a small silver tray beside a dish of nuts then, carrying everything over to the fireplace, offered the child a glass. "Here's to a very good time with my new friend Melanie. *Joyeux noël, ma chère.*"

"I don't expect you'll have much time for me when the parties start."

"You mean, there are no parties for young ladies at Topaz Valley? No singing or dancing or wearing pretty dresses to celebrate the season?"

"Well, they have a Santa Claus for the kids on Christmas morning, but it's really McBride with a pillow stuffed under his coat." The girl gazed at her drink pensively. "I stopped believing in Santa Claus when my mom died and I almost hate Christmas now because it makes me feel so lonely. I'd rather be by myself with our two dogs."

Claire's heart contracted with pity. Even the death of an uncaring mother left a hole in a child's life, as she very well knew, but when that mother had showered her daughter in love, as Melanie's so clearly had, how much more acutely the loss must be felt.

"Well, this year will be different, I promise you. This year, we will have fun." She took the wine goblet from the child and drew her to her feet. "Here, kick off your boots and let's dance."

After a moment's hesitation, Melanie flushed with pleasure and the mouth which at first had been so solemn curved with laughter. Her eyes were sapphire stars, alive with excitement as only a child's can be.

Again, emotion tugged at Claire's heart. How little it took to please the girl, and what she would have given to have just such a daughter herself, someone to spoil a little and love and spend special time with—all those things which had been missing from her relationship with her own mother.

But that was not possible until she'd found the right man with whom to share such joy. Not for her the casual liaison, the unthinking act that brought an unwanted child into the world. First, there had to be a husband, and love strong enough to last a lifetime.

Blinking back sudden, inexplicable tears, she held out her hands to Melanie. "Come, darling. The music's going to waste."

They galloped the length of the room and back again, stumbling a little and laughing a lot until a thump on the door brought them both to a sudden stop. Claire shrugged and smiled. "What did I tell you? Already we're famous for the fun we have and someone else wants to join our party. Turn down the music a little and enjoy your drink, *chérie*, while I see who's so impatient to be let in."

It was Zachary Alexander, his scowl very firmly in place. Did he sleep like that, Claire wondered, with his mouth drawn like a purse string and his winged brows almost meeting above the bridge of his handsome nose?

Determined not to be intimidated by his obviously sour mood, she smiled and said, "How nice to see you again so soon, Mr. Alexander. Won't you come in?"

"This isn't a social call, Miss Durocher."

"Nonetheless, it's too cold to stand on one's dignity out there." She opened the door wider and gestured him inside. "Please, whatever business has brought you here, can't we at least conduct it inside where it's warm?"

"If you don't like the cold," he said, following her into the salon, "why did you choose to spend Christmas in this neck of the woods? Surely you knew it wasn't the tropics."

"*Ah, oui,*" she said, preserving her good humor with difficulty, "even I knew that. But I'm sure you haven't come here to give me a geography lesson. So what can I do for you? Have you decided I may not occupy this suite, after all?"

From her place in the middle of the floor, Melanie said, "Uh-oh," in the kind of voice that warned of trouble ahead.

At that, he flicked his very blue gaze past her to the child and in that instant Claire saw the resemblance between the two of them in the stubborn cast of the mouth. "I have come to collect my daughter," he said, his glance sweeping the room and taking note of the boots kicked to one side, the dish of nuts and the two wine goblets with their jewel-colored contents. "She has no business disturbing you and knows better than to impose herself on a guest."

"It's no imposition, I assure you," Claire said firmly. "Melanie is here at my invitation and we'd both like it very much if you'd join us."

"No, thank you." He turned to leave, pausing only long enough to say over his shoulder, "Put your boots on and let's get going, Mel. I have to be back at the lodge in half an hour."

His footsteps stamped out of the suite and back to the other side of the veranda with a vehemence which suggested he would have liked to grind them across the inter-

loper's throat. Shortly thereafter, his own front door
slammed. Truly, the man was *formidable!* As for his daughter, all her animation had died, leaving her little face
pinched with misery and her mouth drooping sullenly as
she trooped obediently in his wake.

And small wonder! Left too much to her own devices,
with only a couple of dogs for company, half the time—it
was no sort of life for a child.

"Well, *ma petite*, things will be different as long I'm
living next door," Claire muttered, clearing away the remains of their celebration. "By the time Christmas is over,
you'll be glad to see me leave, you'll have grown so tired
of me."

But she knew that wasn't true. The girl was dying inside
for want of affection and the feel of strong, loving arms
around her. *As am I,* she thought. *The need to feel cherished
never goes away, but I don't have the heart to tell you that,
sweet child. Sadly, it's something you'll learn on your own,
all too soon.*

The après-ski happy hour was well underway when Zach
walked into the lounge, and if the noise level was anything
to go by, people were having a good time. In itself, this
was always a positive sign because he knew from experience that a successful social program was a key factor in
keeping the resort in the black. But the scene he'd just had
with Melanie had left him with no taste to party and when
his gaze settled on the cause of this latest father-daughter
spat, his mood blackened further.

Claire Durocher leaned against the far end of the bar, all
dolled up in a clinging jumpsuit. Made of some sort of
sparkly black stuff, with a halter neckline which dipped in
a deep vee at the front, it left so little to the imagination
as to be almost indecent.

She'd tied her hair up to show off her long elegant neck and the diamond-studded hoops which swung in her ears like a pair of metronomes every time she turned her head. Which she did often, batting her silly eyelashes at all the attention she was receiving from every man in the joint. Even McBride was making a damn fool of himself, ogling her from his side of the bar where he sat nursing his hot toddy.

"Keep drooling like that and you'll shrink the ends of your mustache," Zach advised him tersely.

"That's one fine figure of a woman, son," McBride drawled, his gaze never wavering. "Yes, sir, one *fine* figure of a woman!"

Zach flung another sidelong glance to where she continued to hold court, gesturing with her hand and showing off the diamonds strung around her dainty wrist. "If brains were what counts, she'd be standing at the end of the line waiting for other people's leftovers!"

Hoisting himself up on a stool, he flagged down the bartender. "Pour me a Scotch, Charlie. And before you say another word," he added, seeing McBride about to chip in with a further two bits' worth of unasked-for comment, "I'm well aware I don't usually start drinking this early in the day, but I've had another go-round with Mel and it's all because of her." He jerked his head in Claire Durocher's direction, a slight enough gesture to pass unnoticed, he'd have thought, but she must have sensed she was being talked about because she glanced up suddenly and locked gazes with him.

The noise in the room grew oddly distant then; muffled almost, as if everyone else had moved off and left him alone with her. Her expression grew sober and altogether too thoughtful for his peace of mind. Belatedly, he realized that there was a brain behind that disturbingly lovely face, and right at that moment, it was working overtime.

Mesmerized, he lifted his glass and took a mouthful of the Scotch. But nothing it could offer compared to the fire suddenly burning in his blood. She needed to be brought to heel, he thought savagely. Where did she get off waltzing into Topaz Valley and upsetting the even tenor of things? And what was wrong with him that, while the thinking part of him declined to tolerate her intrusion into any aspect of his life, another part knew a sudden primitive ache of desire?

He swore under his breath and tossed back the rest of the Scotch. "I'm off to make sure everything's on schedule in the south wing," he told McBride. "You can hold down the fort in here—always assuming you can keep your mind on the job, that is!"

"When did I ever let you down, Zach?" McBride asked mildly, not once taking his eyes off the Durocher creature.

She'd finally grown tired of trying to stare him down and Zach doubted she even noticed his departure. Unaccountably miffed, he strode to the dining room.

Flames from the big fireplace reflected on polished crystal and silver. Pyramids of napkins starched to within an inch of their lives stood to attention beside every plate. Arrangements of chrysanthemums and holly surrounded the candle centerpieces. Sterling serving dishes lined the massive rosewood sideboard he'd bought at a hotel auction. A twelve-foot Noble fir sparkling with Christmas lights stood in one of the window recesses.

Surveying the scene restored his equilibrium somewhat. It was with just such attention to luxury that he'd built Topaz Valley's reputation. There were plenty of ski resorts which catered to a less discriminating crowd, where hamburgers and pots of chili were the order of the day and the baked goods were obtained commercially. But he'd known that if he was to persuade people to undertake the journey to this remote and beautiful place, he had to make it worth their while.

Satisfied that he was succeeding, he passed through the swing doors at the far end of the room and entered the butler's pantry leading to the kitchen. A chalkboard propped against a cabinet showed the evening menu: crab chowder and crusty baguettes, poached pear salad, roast partridge with spiced orange salsa and wild rice, brandied mince tarts, peach compote, and a selection of imported and Canadian cheeses with fresh fruit.

As a peace offering, he'd invited Mel to join him for dinner in the dining room, but she'd insisted she wasn't hungry. Actually, what she'd said was that she'd rather eat dirt, which amounted to the same thing, albeit in less polite terms. Pretty irate himself and feeling perfectly justified in pointing out that she had no business hobnobbing with adult guests in their private quarters, he'd made her grilled cheese sandwiches and left her to sulk at home. Pity she was missing out on her favorite crab chowder, though. Not that she'd exactly starve on grilled cheese, but still...

"Oh, what the hell!" Exasperated, he filled a bowl with soup, swiped some bread, cheese and fruit, and piled the whole lot on a tray. "If I dithered like this in business, I'd be in bankruptcy court within the year," he muttered, heading for the door.

But parenting refused to be cut and dried. Too often, he simply didn't know the best route to take, and as Mel grew older and less tractable, he found himself wondering if he was up to the job of bringing up a daughter single-handedly. He wasn't exactly famous for his insight into the female psyche, after all.

It was still snowing lightly when he went outside a few

minutes later, but a smattering of stars now showed through the ragged cloud cover. The air was sharp as crystal, filled with the scent of pine and fir and wood smoke, and quiet as a church.

He paused a moment at the top of the main lodge steps, just to inhale the fragrant peace. This was what he'd worked for, for the last twelve years and he was nuts to let anything spoil the pleasure of his achievement. The holidays were almost here, more than thirty feet of snow had fallen already, and it would take a lot more than a spat over a temporary guest to come between him and his daughter and spoil their Christmas together.

The easiest route to the house was by the path which was always kept plowed for the convenience of visitors, but for anyone familiar with the lay of the land, the fastest way was to hike through the trees and come out on the other side of the property near the hot tub.

Rapping on the family room window as he passed by, he called out, "It's only me, honey."

"How come you're back so soon?" Mel asked, letting him in the side door. "I thought you were staying at the lodge for dinner."

"I brought you a few treats," he said, setting the tray on the kitchen table.

"No, thanks." Barely glancing at it, she returned to the couch and plunked herself back in front of the TV. "I already had some."

"I hardly call grilled cheese sandwiches special," he said, determined not to let the rift widen between them. "Come on, Mel, at least look at what I've brought for you."

"Honestly, Dad, I'm not hungry." She indicated the crumbs left on the plate beside her. "Claire already brought me some snacks from the cocktail party."

"Why did she feel the need to do that?" he asked evenly.

"She felt sorry for me being left up here all by myself. She doesn't think I have enough fun."

"Is that a fact?" he said, wondering how high a man's blood pressure could go before he fell victim to a sudden stroke or heart attack. "And does she also think you're half-starved? Is that why she brought you extra food?"

Mel shrugged. "I dunno. She didn't give a reason."

Not to you, perhaps, he fumed, *but she'll damned well explain herself to me!* Aloud, he said, "I thought we had a rule, Mel. You don't open the door to strangers."

"She's not a stranger, she's my friend."

"You can't possibly know that on such short acquaintance."

His daughter might still have the face of a child but the eyes she turned his way were full of mysterious female wisdom. "Time doesn't have anything to do with it, Dad. Sometimes, two people just click."

Oh, brother! Helplessly, he ran a hand through his hair. "We'll talk about this in the morning. Right now, I want your word that you're not going to open that door to anyone else tonight. I won't be late and I'll let myself in when I come home."

She rolled her eyes. "I suppose you want me in bed by nine, as well?"

"Keep up the smart mouth, miss, and you'll be in bed by eight!"

Sudden tears glittered in her eyes and her chin trembled uncontrollably. "On the other hand," he went on, utterly defeated, "it is Christmas and I did say you could stay up until ten. Just don't push your luck, okay?"

"Okay, Daddy."

He buried a sigh and tramping back the way he'd come,

wondered if any other word in the English language was calculated to melt a man's heart the way "daddy" did. He'd walk through fire for his little girl; slay dragons, battle monsters and lay down his life for her, if he had to. What he wouldn't do, though, was stand aside and let the busybody from next door march in and take over.

"One moment, Miss Durocher," he said, coming into the lounge and cornering her as the rest of the guests began drifting toward the dining room. "I've got something I'd like to say to you."

"Really?" she said, in the sort of surprised tone that suggested she didn't think him capable of stringing together more than two words at a stretch.

Somehow, up close, her jumpsuit didn't seem quite as daring. Just very...attractive. He cleared his throat. "Yes. Specifically, I want to know on whose authority you decided to take a hand in my daughter's upbringing."

She had quite the most extraordinary eyes he'd ever come across. Large and gray, and enhanced by lashes that were almost certainly not her own, they dominated her delicate face. They focused on him now with the intent curiosity of a scientist inspecting a new, rather low form of alien life. "I'm not sure I understand what you mean."

"Then let me be more direct. Butt out of my business, particularly as it relates to Melanie."

She blinked, doing a slow-motion sweep with those ridiculous lashes in such a way that she managed to turn a perfectly ordinary action into something absurdly distracting. "Is this because I invited her to visit me in my chalet, or because I thought to share a few of my excellent hors d'oeuvres with her?"

"Both," he snapped.

"But why? Where's the harm?"

"First of all, it's ridiculous that a guest feel obliged to

leave a social function in order to look in on someone else's child, let alone bring her food as if she was a foundling left on the doorstep. And second—"

"But I didn't leave the party for that reason. I was feeling a little chilled and realized I had forgotten my wrap, so I went back to get it."

That was why the jumpsuit looked different! The matching shawl she'd flung around her shoulders covered all the pale, translucent flesh he'd noticed earlier, rendering her marginally less exposed. "I see."

"Do you?" she said, laughing a little. "I wonder. You look at me so suspiciously, Mr. Alexander, as if you think I might try to corrupt your little one with my wicked, foreign ways. But I assure you, taking her a few inconsequential appetizers was an afterthought, an impulse only, and certainly not intended to cause you such distress."

She made him feel like a fool, like some gauche country bumpkin who didn't know how to handle himself with a woman, and he resented it. Placing his hand in the small of her back and urging her toward the dining room, he said, "Well, do me a favor and curb your impulses in future, Miss Durocher. You're here to enjoy the winter sports and hospitality, not assume responsibility for my daughter."

"I enjoy her company. It's no hardship to spend time with her."

"You're missing the point."

"Am I?" she said, practically cooing the question at him. "And what point is that, Mr. Alexander?"

"That if I find myself in need of a baby-sitter, there are plenty on hand without my having to seek help from a visitor. Oh, and one more thing. Unlike the public guest accommodations, your suite isn't equipped with its own safe. Although my staff is handpicked and utterly trustworthy, you'd be well advised to leave your jewelry in the office safe when you're not wearing it. The management of the resort is not responsible for valuables carelessly left lying around."

Unaccountably, she laughed again and shook her braceleted wrist under his nose. "You mean this?" she gurgled, as if they were discussing something found in a box of Cracker Jack.

The woman was too cute for her own good and so filthy rich that she probably wouldn't give a hoot if she accidentally flushed a few diamonds down the toilet, but he was damned if he was going to be held accountable for it! Skewering her in a glare, he said, "Suit yourself, Ms. Durocher, as long as you're aware that, in the event of any mishaps, it'll be your loss, not mine."

Mon dieu, she thought, shivering as she watched him stalk away, the man was colder than the weather outside, and slightly mad to boot. Surely he had not built such success as he obviously enjoyed by treating all his guests so rudely?

Throughout the dinner, she secretly watched him. He sat several tables removed from hers, too far for her to hear what he said but close enough that she could see the smile he turned on others and how he charmed them with his wit and humor.

The knowledge had an odd effect on her. He was a stranger, after all, and would play no lasting part in her life. Yet his rejection, for surely that was what it was, hurt her. It touched too closely on that part of her life she had left behind, reminding her of events best forgotten.

Determinedly, she turned her attention to the people at her own table. She hadn't traveled so many miles to let one man spoil her time here. Yes, she had been hasty in assuming the unavailability of the suite she'd reserved was the result of mismanagement, but when she had learned the real reason, she had accepted it with grace. If he could not extend to her the same courtesy and forgive her for her oversight, she would ignore him. If she could.

Sadly, though, he was not a man easily overlooked. Nor was she the only one to think so. At dinner's end, he went from table to table, inquiring of his guests if the meal had met their expectations, and she saw how he was greeted. On the one hand, he was what people called a man's man, respected for his intelligence and capability.

But what she noticed most was how the women behaved. How those who were unattached looked at him with hungry eyes; how they managed to draw his attention with a little touch on the arm, an inviting smile. She noticed, too, how he responded, acknowledging their unspoken messages without promising anything—except when he stopped at the table where she sat, and his glance slid over her as if she were invisible, and filled with interest only when he moved on to the person beside her.

So he knew how to be charming as well as anyone, she thought, annoyed by such overt and unwarranted discourtesy. He just did not want to be charming to her.

Well, she would change his mind! Before this Christmas was over, Zachary Alexander would discover that there was more to Claire Durocher than the self-indulgent, empty-headed creature he was determined to make her out to be. By the time she left Topaz Valley, she would have earned his respect, if not his admiration. He might even end up being sorry to see her leave!

CHAPTER THREE

SHE should have slept long and soundly that night. Snug beneath the thick down quilt, with the firelight painting hypnotic shadows on the walls and nothing but the deep, black silence of the Canadian night outside, she should have succumbed to the exhaustion of travel and an inner clock not yet adjusted to the nine-hour time difference between Europe and B.C.

Instead, she awoke before sunrise, her mind sharp and eager, and her body filled with restless energy. And why? Because, the night before, Zachary Alexander had almost kissed her.

Almost...

She had timed her after-dinner departure from the lodge to coincide with his and since they were, as he'd so reluctantly conceded, next-door neighbors, he'd had little choice but to accept her company on the walk back to the house.

"Watch you don't slip," he ordered, as they navigated the steps leading from the lodge to the lakeshore path. "It's very icy underfoot."

Small wonder! The wind had dropped, a mercy to be sure, but still the air knifed into her lungs. Shivering despite the quilted lining of her ankle-length coat, Claire had clutched the collar to her throat and glanced covertly at her companion.

He seemed unaffected by the cold but then, from all she'd seen, he was more than a match for it. Profile unreadable, he'd marched along, making little concession to her shorter stride.

"Your chef served an excellent dinner," she said, gasping to keep pace.

"Yes."

"The partridge was particularly delicious."

He grunted.

"By itself almost worth the journey over here."

"Uh-huh."

"The lights," she said, skidding a little as they hit a particularly slippery spot, "look very pretty strung through the trees, don't you think?"

Another grunt, half buried in an exasperated sigh, at which her own irritation rose to boiling point.

"How is it that you find so much to say to others and yet have so little to say to me, Mr. Alexander? Am I so reprehensible?"

He spared her a glance, one which swept from her hair piled high on her head to her feet in their fur-lined doeskin boots. The effect reminded her of a raindrop falling down a windowpane and freezing before it reached the bottom. "I have no feelings for you one way or the other, Miss Durocher."

She laughed. "And there are roses growing on the moon!"

"You think I'm lying?"

"Perhaps. Or perhaps you're afraid of me."

He also laughed then, a sound so full of scorn that she shriveled inside. "Why on earth would I be afraid of you?"

"Because," she said rashly, "I disturb your peace. I threaten your authority. And most of all, I distract you. You pretend to ignore me yet all the time, you're watching me. You're like a moth drawn to my flame."

This time, his laughter was genuine, rolling out into the

night like fire-warmed cognac. "You flatter yourself, Miss Durocher."

"And you call me miss, but refer to everyone else by their first names."

"You call me mister," he sneered. "Should I take that to mean you're irresistibly drawn to my flame, too?"

They had reached the house. The steps which gave onto the veranda were so treacherous with crystals of new-fallen snow that, by accident, she stumbled against him. And because, despite his brusque manner, he was at heart a gentleman, he caught her securely by the arm and attempted to steady her.

But he hated having to do it and pushed her away too abruptly. At that, they both lost their footing and for a moment slithered together in graceless confusion, clutching at empty air, before landing in the deep snow piled beside the path.

It was fluffy as goose down, cushioning their fall at the same time that it imprisoned them in its softness. Try though he might to extricate himself with dignity from the hollow they'd created when they fell, he could find no purchase. Snowflakes clung to his hair, slid inside the collar of his jacket, swallowed his feet.

"You did that on purpose!" he said, infuriated by the gurgle of amusement which escaped her.

Batting her eyelashes and trying hard to look properly rebuked, she murmured, "But how is that possible? You are so big and strong and I am but a weak little woman! Zachary, you give me too much credit."

They were half-lying together, so closely that the fog of his breath touched sweetly against her face. So closely that she saw how his gaze lingered on her laughing mouth.

A strange longing swept over her at that, a sense almost of confronting a destiny so full of promise that not to nurture it was to waste a gift from the gods. She could have forgiven him his surliness then, and might even have dared to let him see the uncertain, tender side of her which she too often hid for fear of being laughed at, if he had shown her a little gentleness.

But he did not. Instead, he hauled himself upright and growled, "Save that routine for some other fool. It's wasted on me."

"*Zut!*" she exclaimed, and spat out a mouthful of snow. "I was teasing you, for heaven's sake! Is that any reason to leave me here to freeze? Come, Zachary, surely even you wouldn't stoop so low?"

He let out such an explosive breath of annoyance that, for a moment, she wondered if he might go so far as to bury her and hope no one found her until the spring thaw. But the reluctant knight in him came to the fore. With ill-concealed exasperation, he leaned down, grabbed her hand and yanked her clear of the snowbank. Did it so forcefully that she found herself flying through the air and coming to rest pressed up against his formidable frame with the breath knocked out of her.

They remained so for a small eternity, knee to knee and breast to breast, he panting a little and she gasping. So close were they that she could feel his heart thumping through the layers of his clothing. Or was it hers suddenly running amok? Because, this near, he was even more beautiful than at a distance. Such smooth olive skin he had, such elegance of design in the angled slash of his cheekbones, such strength of character in the iron set of his jaw.

I could enjoy being kissed by him, she'd thought dreamily, and felt herself swaying toward him. How heavy her eyelids had felt all at once, how languorous her limbs.

That was when he'd almost kissed her. His mouth had hovered so close to hers that the outline of his face had blurred in her vision. She could almost taste the cold firm texture of his lips. She even went so far as to lift a hand to caress his cheek.

Wary creature that he was, though, he saw the danger and reared back. "Why did you have to come here for Christmas? Why couldn't you have stayed in Switzerland, the farther away from me, the better."

She flinched at such an attack. "What is it about me that irritates you so much?"

"As if you don't know!" Sudden color slashed his high cheekbones, matched by the light of awareness in his eyes of a man confronting dangerous temptation. "Just keep away from me before I give you what you're asking for," he growled and, surefooted despite the icy conditions, took the steps two at a time.

Without waiting to see if she made it safely inside hers, he'd disappeared through his own front door as if he were escaping a fate too treacherous to be endured....

Just then, a swath of lamplight spilled out from next door and flung a reflection against her window. The clock on the bedside table showed six-thirty. Already thoroughly awake, Claire threw back the comforter, slipped into her robe and went into the main salon, the living room as they called it in Canada.

Although the fire had burned low, enough embers remained for a handful of kindling to revive them. She threw in another log, turned on the stereo, and then, since breakfast would not be served in the lodge for at least another hour, she plugged in the coffeemaker before heading for the shower.

When she returned to the room some forty-five minutes later, the fire was blazing merrily and the air laced with the aroma of French roasted coffee. Pouring a cup, she carried it to the window and drew back the curtains.

"Oh, but this is magnificent...!" she breathed, staring out in wonder.

Not a thing remained of yesterday's gray gloom. Overnight, the cloud had lifted and left the sky a pale and tender mauve against which the stars winked faintly. This side of the house, she realized, also looked out on the frozen lake and, as she watched, the still invisible sun cast a rosy stain on the tips of the mountain ridge on the east horizon.

It had snowed a little more during the night, an inch or two only, just enough to lay an unblemished veil of white over a small lower deck where, she noticed for the first time, stood a whirlpool encircled in glass to protect bathers from the wind.

Clasping her coffee cup in both hands, she gave a little sigh of pleasure. This was what she'd hoped to find when she'd fled Europe: a northern paradise, peaceful, remote, pristine, and just a little intimidating in its untamed splendor.

All at once, a movement caught her eye as a door opened in the other part of the house and Zachary Alexander stepped into view. From behind the curtains, Claire watched as he went down to the whirlpool and lifted its cover.

At once, clouds of steam escaped and hung motionless in the still air. Stooping, he pulled a thermometer from the water and inspected it then, seeming satisfied, dropped it back into the tub and replaced the cover. But instead of returning to the house, he stood with his back to the building and surveyed his tiny kingdom.

What a sight he made! Slim-fitting black slacks hugged his long, strong legs, a heavy black sweater decorated with a single red racing stripe showcased his broad shoulders, and beneath it, in dazzling contrast to his deep winter tan, he wore a white shirt.

Idly, he pushed back a lock of hair which had fallen across his brow as he bent over the spa, then flung a glance over his shoulder as if he knew he was being watched. Instinctively, Claire ducked behind the curtain only to realize a second later that it was not at her that he was looking but at Melanie who, wearing only a pair of boots and her pajamas, had come out to speak to her father.

Claire couldn't hear what was said but it was obvious that, whatever the topic, he wasn't prepared to discuss it in the snow. Loping up the steps, he hurried his daughter inside. The outer door closed, followed by the slamming of another door which even the thick inner walls of the building couldn't quite muffle. And then voices, the father's deep and calm, but the girl's high and angry.

A few minutes later, Claire saw him leave again, this time by the front door, and strike out along the path toward the lodge. Apparently discouraged by his altercation with Melanie, he strode along, head down and shoulders hunched despondently.

Astonishingly, Claire felt a stab of pity for the man. Whatever his faults, and clearly he had many, he was obviously devoted to his child. At the same time, he seemed at a loss to know how best to deal with her, and who could wonder? Trying to fill the role of both parents was difficult enough, but to be the father at odds with a teenage girl...!

And Melanie herself, how alone and confused she must feel, half-child and half-adult as she was, and not sure in which world she truly belonged. Perhaps it would help if she could talk to another woman. Hadn't she admitted as much, just yesterday?

Slipping on her jacket, Claire stepped outside and

knocked on the other front door. "What are your plans for the morning?" she asked, when Melanie answered. "Can you spare a little time for a new friend and teach her which runs are the best for skiing?"

Ten minutes later, they were on their way to the lodge for breakfast. "You look so cool, the way you dress and do your hair, and stuff," Melanie said, gazing at her admiringly. "And the way you talk—sort of like French women do in the movies. I don't know what I can teach you. You must know just about everything."

"Not everything, *ma petite,* but enough to see that you're not always as happy as you should be. For instance, when you opened the door to me just now, you looked very sad."

"I had another fight with my dad." She made a droll face. "We fight every day lately, mostly because I want to go to boarding school and he wants to keep me stuck here in the valley where he can keep an eye on me."

"That's natural enough, surely? Most fathers want to protect their daughters."

"You mean, you had the same trouble with your dad when you were thirteen?"

The question caught Claire off guard. "My father was...not there then. I had only my mother."

"Uh-oh!" Sensitive to Claire's changed tone, Melanie looked apprehensive. "Sorry if I said something I shouldn't."

"You didn't. I grew up without a father, that's all. Just as you are having to grow up without your mother."

At the mention of her mother, Melanie's mouth drooped sadly. Cursing herself for not thinking before she spoke, Claire slipped her arm around the child's narrow shoulders. "You miss her very much, don't you, darling?"

"Yeah, especially at Christmas."

"I'm sure she misses you, too, and wishes she could be with you."

"You think so?" The eyes were huge and much too bereft for one so young.

"I'm certain of it. A mother never willingly forsakes her babies, no matter where they might be or how old they are."

It wasn't true, of course. If it were, surely her own childhood would have been different. But how could she destroy Melanie with such knowledge? Better to tell a little lie, especially when it produced such a shining smile.

What with the almost daily influx of new guests and the final countdown to Christmas, the rest of the week was even busier than usual, leaving Zach with little time to spare. For that reason alone, he ought to have been grateful that Mel had found someone to keep her company while he attended to business. Instead, he found himself seething with resentment.

Any time he *was* able to spend with his daughter always followed the same pattern. She'd bombard him with everything there was to know about Claire Durocher, all delivered with the sort of rapt attention to detail of a kid with a serious case of hero worship. *Claire thinks…Claire says…Claire knows…Claire's met…Claire's got…*

The plain truth was, he'd had it up to here with Claire Durocher and her opinions. She could be kissing cousins with every royal house in Europe for all he cared. She still didn't have a clue when it came to what was best for his daughter.

He was sick of seeing Mel joined at the hip with the woman. Trying to pry her loose was worse than scraping barnacles off a rock and damn it, he shouldn't have to try! He was her father, he had rights—but who cared? Not that infernal French creature! It had taken God seven days to make the world but she'd only needed five to turn it on its ear!

"She burns my wires!" he'd exploded to McBride, at one point.

"That ain't all she's burnin'," McBride had chortled. "You got the hots for the woman, but you're too dang stubborn to admit it."

It wasn't true. And even if it were, he came too saddled with responsibility to capture the lasting attention of a woman like Claire Durocher. Nor was he prepared to stand by and watch her wreak havoc on Mel's life.

Which was why, on the morning of the twenty-third, he stood hidden by the potted Norfolk Island pine just inside the door of the foyer, feeling like a two-bit spy in a third-rate movie as he watched the two of them deep in conversation as they approached the lodge. What secrets were they sharing? And why did Mel find it so easy to confide in a total stranger instead of him?

A feeling he was becoming all too familiar with caught him off guard again, stabbing at him with gleeful spite. Jealousy, that's what it was, and it had begun the day Claire Durocher had marched into their lives in her smart little Italian leather après-ski boots and taken up her spot at center stage. But the disturbing question was, of whom was he jealous? The woman—or his daughter?

The question lodged in his stomach with all the comfort of a lead cannonball. The notion was ridiculous! And he was a fool to waste a moment of his valuable time debating its validity.

They came bounding up the steps just then, giggling like a pair of kids. Mel's coltish awkwardness was disguised by her down parka and calf-high boots, and the other one looked elegant as a dancer in her fancy European duds.

He watched, and he hated the pettiness Claire Durocher brought out in him. When was the last time Mel had looked at him like that, as if the sun rose and set on his slightest word? When had her expression last been so open and eager?

Claire Durocher caught sight of him and trilled a sunny *"Bonjour!"* as if she was quite used to finding grown men hiding behind strategically placed potted Norfolk Island pines.

"Good morning," he acknowledged, trying to match her breezy informality, and winced at the way his words tumbled out stiff with resentment. He'd never thought himself a possessive man but there was no denying the reason he reached for Melanie and drew her away from her new friend and into the curve of his arm. "Hi, sweetheart. I was looking forward to having a quiet breakfast with you, but you're kind of late and I'm a bit pressed for time."

"It doesn't matter," she said, wriggling away from him. "I've got Claire to keep me company."

The effort nearly choked him but he managed to bare his teeth in a smile. "Just as well, because I've already eaten and I'm meeting McBride down at the stable in a few minutes. But maybe we can team up for a couple of runs down the back hill before lunch."

"We? You mean, you and me and Claire?"

The hollandaise sauce on the eggs Benedict he'd eaten half an hour before must have been off. Why else did he feel like throwing up? "If you like."

Claire Durocher fixed him in a penetrating gaze. "But what would *you* like, Mr. Alexander?"

Her ski suit was dark blue, the exact color of a clear northern sky just before darkness fell, and the turquoise sweater she wore underneath made her skin glow like warm ivory. Her hair curled softly against her neck, dark and thick and lustrous as satin.

It had been a long time since he'd run his fingers through a woman's hair....

Abruptly, he shut out the thought. There'd been too many like it popping into his mind in the last few days. What he would like didn't bear thinking about, not if it involved Claire Durocher—and it always seemed to, lately. Waking or sleeping, she was in his face twenty-four hours a day.

"I don't wish to intrude," she said, when he offered no reply to her question.

"You're not," Melanie piped up. "Dad and I can ski by ourselves any old time."

"Then you're very lucky, *chérie*." Gravely, the woman reached forward to tuck a strand of Mel's hair behind her ear and, inevitably, he found his gaze drawn to the slender, aristocratic fingers with their immaculately painted nails. "Most fathers are too busy to be able to spend extra time with their daughters."

Melanie shot him an urgent glare. "Tell her it's okay to come with us, Dad!"

Cornered and seeing no means of escape, he shrugged. "Sure," he said, too heartily. With the pair of them staring at him like starving urchins, what other choice did he have but to agree? "I'll meet you at the top of the lift at eleven."

"I look forward to it," Claire Durocher said, and tilted her head toward the dining room. "Won't you at least join us for coffee, Mr. Alexander? I know we'd both enjoy it."

We'd both enjoy it. As if he were the interloper!

Burying his irritation, he glanced at his watch. "I suppose I can spare a few more minutes."

"Why do you call him Mr. Alexander?" Melanie asked

her, when they were seated. "Why don't you just call him Zach, like everyone else?"

She wrapped her elegant hands around her café au lait bowl and swung that luminous, dark-lashed stare at him once again, seeming to look clear into his mind and discerning a great deal more than he wanted her to know. "Because he calls me Miss Durocher."

Mees, she said, enunciating the word in such a way that it was transformed from ordinary to exotic. Melanie gazed at her, entranced, then glared at him accusingly. "Tell her, Dad."

"Tell her what?" He shifted uneasily in his seat and made a big production of stirring his coffee, which was pretty silly considering he took it without sugar or cream.

"That it's okay to call you Zach, of course. Then you can call her Claire."

"Of course it's okay," he said, sounding like a trained parrot. "So, tell me, er, Claire, what made you decide to come to Topaz Valley? It's a bit off the beaten path for Europeans, especially when you've got some of the best skiing in the world right on your own doorstep."

"I was ready for a change." She nibbled at her croissant, swallowed thoughtfully and tilted one shoulder in a dismissive shrug. "After a while, even St. Moritz becomes dull."

"So you decided to come slumming to North America for a change." He didn't attempt to hide his sarcasm, which earned him another black glare from Melanie.

"No, Zachary," Claire said slyly, regarding him from beneath the sweep of her lashes. "I came here looking for something quite different and I do believe I might have found it."

He didn't like the gut reaction that triggered in him—the flare of sexual awareness which was becoming all too familiar—and he didn't like her. Nor did he trust her. She was filling Melanie's head with too many cockamamie ideas. Already his tomboy daughter was imitating her table manners, sticking out her pinky as she hefted her mug of hot chocolate and dabbing daintily at her mouth with her napkin. She'd be speaking French next.

He said as much to McBride when he met him in the stables shortly after, and in return got a lecture on adolescent psychology and how a girl needed to bond with a woman—all from a man who'd never been married, let alone fathered a child!

"Things could be worse," McBride had concluded. "She could've latched on to a boy, instead. Now that would be trouble! Or didn't you never grab the chance to roll around in a snowdrift with a good-looking little gal and just kinda check out by accident how God put her together?"

Just as recently as last week, now that you come to mention it, Zach thought and, to his intense annoyance, felt a flush ride over his face. In the space of the two minutes or however long it had taken him to climb out of the snowbank, the night she'd arrived, he'd learned that Claire Durocher was soft where a woman was meant to be soft, firm in all the right places, and with the kind of curves guaranteed to drive a man crazy. Which was what he must have been to have come so close to kissing her.

"Why don't you stick to what you get paid to do, McBride?" he snapped. "Extra bales of straw have to be hauled down for tonight's sleigh ride. The warming huts' supplies need restocking. The trees for the guest house verandas still have to be cut." He shot a furious glance at his trusty man Friday. "I take it you've assigned someone to take care of all that? And that we've got enough strings of lights to go around and you've seen to it that any burned out bulbs have been replaced?"

"Yup." McBride grinned evilly. "All except yours, sonny boy! The way you're carryin' on, I reckon you're about ready for a complete rewirin'."

Zach scowled. "The season of goodwill's got a real stranglehold on you this year, hasn't it, McBride?" he muttered sourly and stamped off before he said something he'd really regret.

Claire paused at the crest of a steep slope and leaned on her ski poles a moment to admire the view while she waited for Melanie to catch up with her.

All around, the mountain peaks reached up to meet the great dome of the sky spreading in endless blue to the far reaches of the world, while below, like a toy village cupped in a child's hand, lay the resort. The air was so clear and sparkling that even from this distance she could see the sun glinting off the windows of the lodge and the tiny figures skating on the lake.

Melanie carved a neat turn and skied to a stop beside her. "It's almost eleven, Claire, and we'd better get going or Dad'll be sending out a search party for us. He's really strict about people showing up when they're supposed to and gets madder than a bear with a sore paw when he rounds up the ski patrol for nothing because someone forgot to check in at the base. Come on, I'll race you."

She planted her poles in the snow and pushed off, leaving Claire to trail behind. She'd been taught well and her father should be proud. On skis she was transformed from an awkward adolescent to a graceful bird in flight.

He was waiting for them when they arrived at the lift station but he wasn't alone and, with a squeal of excitement, Melanie rushed up to fling herself at the man standing beside him. "You came after all!" she cried, getting all tangled up in his skis and poles.

"Well, sure," the man replied, pulling her toque down over her eyes teasingly. "You didn't think I'd miss the best turkey Christmas dinner in Canada, did you?"

"But you were supposed to get here last weekend!"

He peeled back the cuff of her toque and planted a kiss on her nose. "I know, pumpkin, and I'm sorry I'm late. Something came up—you know how it is around this time of year—but I'm here now and ready to make up for lost time."

He was tall, though not as tall as Zachary, with light brown hair, blue eyes full of laughter and an open, friendly face. When he noticed Claire, he raised his eyebrows flirtatiously and said to Melanie, "Who's this other pretty lady, Miss Alexander, or don't you want me to know?"

"She's Claire and she's French but she speaks English. And she's my friend." Melanie's face was flushed with excitement as she turned to include Claire in the group. "This is Eric Baxter, my favorite man in the whole world, Claire."

For an unguarded moment, a bereft hurting flickered in Zachary Alexander's dark blue eyes, and Claire felt a stab of sympathy. But he recovered quickly. "What Melanie forgot to mention, Claire, is that Eric is also her uncle and my late wife's brother. Miss Durocher is a guest at the resort, Eric, and I'm afraid she's taken over your usual quarters."

"So I've been told." Eric Baxter's warm gaze traveled a leisurely path from her head to her toes and back again. "Nice to meet you, Claire."

Zachary's mouth tightened with displeasure. Glancing at his watch, he said abruptly, "We've hardly got time to ski down to the base now. It's getting too close to lunch and I want to be there early to oversee things."

"Why don't you ride the chair down then?" Melanie said offhandedly. "We can ski the back run without you."

"Okay. I'll see you back at the lodge." He shrugged and turned away, quietly accepting his daughter's unfeeling dismissal.

"Come on, Claire, let's go!" Melanie gestured impatiently.

But Claire couldn't draw her gaze away from the solitary figure cutting the edge of his skis into the slope and climbing the ramp to the chair lift, and her heart bled for him. "Go ahead without me," she said, waving the girl on her way. "I'm rather tired and think I'll ride down with your father."

She caught up with him just as the next empty chair swung around the tower. In seconds, they were scooped up and lifted high into the air, as alone as if they were the only two people on the mountain.

He pushed his goggles up onto the crown of his toque and she knew he was looking at her, his blue eyes serious and inquiring, and that he was waiting for her to explain her sudden decision to choose his company over Melanie's and her easy, charming uncle's.

And for once, she was at a loss to explain. All she knew was that the crisp cold air numbed her cheeks and made her eyes water. Yet being close to him filled her with a sweet warmth and if she hadn't known better, she'd have thought they were real tears stinging her eyes. And why? Because she knew he was hurting, and that hurt her, too.

It was not a comfortable sensation at all.

CHAPTER FOUR

SHE swallowed and searched for something to say—anything to break the tense silence stretching between them. But he was the one to end it finally. "I'm probably going to regret asking this, but what's going on? Why aren't you skiing the back bowl with the other two?"

She thought about making up excuses. *My boots are hurting. I was too nervous. The slope looked too difficult.* And knew he'd see them for the lies they were because he was no fool. He knew she skied the Swiss Alps, that her equipment was the best. Yet for her to come out with the truth and say that she felt sorry for him for the way his daughter had shut him out was unthinkable. She had known him a little less than a week, but that was time enough to recognize him as a proud man. He would neither welcome nor tolerate her pity.

"I felt in the way," she said, steering a safe middle course. "A third wheel, as you say in English."

Surprisingly, he laughed. "It's fifth wheel, actually, but I know where you're coming from. As far as Mel's concerned, the sun rises and sets on Eric and when he shows up, everyone else fades into the background. Not only is he the big brother she always wanted, but she's at an impressionable age. Movie star good looks, fast cars, and a devil-may-care attitude carry a lot of weight with her these days."

"But he's not her father. You're the one she knows she can always rely on."

"That's me, all right," he said wryly. "Dull but dependable."

Not so, she thought. There were hidden layers beneath his outer reserve; hidden fires. Hadn't she been singed by their heat already, despite her best efforts to remain untouched? The brother-in-law's flame might appear to burn more brightly but it would quickly die without an audience to fuel it. A woman would have long forgotten Eric Baxter's name before she'd begun to plumb Zachary Alexander's depths.

Perhaps she would tell him that before her time in the valley was over, but not yet. Not until he showed himself willing to scratch beneath *her* surface and discover someone other than a rich, self-centered woman with too much idle time on her hands. "It's not easy trying to be father and mother to a child," she said.

"How do you know?" He angled a sideways glance at her. "Have you ever tried it?"

She shook her head. "No. I've never been married."

"The two don't necessarily follow in this day and age."

"They do for me," she said firmly. "I'm not willing to settle for half a loaf of bread, nor will I ask a child to do so."

"And what if you're not given the option? What if one parent dies, as my wife did, or simply tires of the role and walks out on the job?"

"Then, of course, one must manage alone, even though..."

"Even though what?" he prompted, when she didn't continue. "Even though it's only second best?"

"I was going to say, even though, for a man left alone to bring up a daughter, it must be especially difficult."

"Is that your way of telling me I'm falling down on the job?" She felt his stare, his hostility, and knew he was challenging her to look him in the face and refute the allegation.

She should have known better than to think subtlety or innuendo would sneak unnoticed past a man of his keen perceptions. Or to hope, when she didn't immediately answer, that he'd be gallant enough to direct the conversation elsewhere. Slowly, she turned her head and locked gazes with him. "Perhaps."

He exhaled, a short, sharp breath of annoyance. "In what respect—or is a week's acquaintance not quite long enough for you to have figured that out?"

"Melanie's not as…finely tuned in the art of femininity as she might be."

"The art of femininity?" He made no effort to disguise his scorn. "What the hell is that supposed to mean? That she's not like you?"

"She's not, no, nor—"

"Small wonder! She wasn't born with a silver spoon in her mouth or brought up to think the rest of the world exists only to please her."

"I was going to say, if you'd let me finish, nor should she have to be like me, or anyone else, for that matter. She is herself, and charming. As for my childhood, you don't know me nearly well enough to judge me so harshly, Zachary."

"I know a spoiled brat when I meet one."

She sighed. "What must I do to erase your first impression of me? Scrub floors? Beg forgiveness for allowing fatigue to gain the upper hand and make me short-tempered over an unavoidable change of accommodation plans? If so, I'm begging. Mea culpa, a thousand times." She reached for his gloved hand and pressed her mouth briefly to the back of his fingers. "There! I'd kiss your feet but they're out of reach, so that will have to do."

She thought he'd wrench his hand away but he didn't. Instead, he rested it beneath her chin and tilted her face to his. "You don't have to go quite that far," he muttered, his wonderful blue eyes gazing into hers. "Come to that, I've been a bit out of line myself. I don't usually make a habit of haranguing guests but you…" His glance drifted to her mouth and lingered there. "You touched a nerve with your remark about…about…"

"Oui?" The word ghosted into the air on a puff of vapor, expelled on a breath so labored that her lungs burned. How was it that, with a simple look, a touch, he could create such chaos within her? Other men didn't. But he— oh, he turned her liquid with need! She felt herself yearning toward him, aching to know the sweet, cold taste of his lips on hers.

Recognizing the danger, he shifted his weight away from her to the other side of the chair. "There's no question Mel misses her mother, just as I miss my wife, and I'm not so arrogant as to think it doesn't show. Nor am I too proud to accept well-intended advice from the people closest to us. You don't happen to be one of them, that's all."

"What if your daughter thinks I am? What if she turns to me with questions she can't bring to you? Would you have me ignore her?"

He thumped one fist rhythmically against the armrest at his side and expelled another breath laden with exasperation. "I guess not," he said, from between his teeth. "But I'd prefer that you not encourage her to confide in you."

"Why not?"

They were approaching the foot of the lift. "Because there's no point in her becoming attached to someone who'll be gone in another week," he said, gathering his poles into one hand. "A month from now, you'll be just another name on our mailing list. A year from now, it's unlikely we'll be able to put a face to that name. To put it very bluntly, Claire, you have no lasting relevance in our lives.''

After lunch, Darcy, his recreational program director, organized activities on the lake, including skating and games for the adults and older children, and rides for the youngsters with Blanche and Lily towing a toboggan. Work permitting, he'd normally have spent an hour or two taking part in the fun. Not only did guests expect the boss to make an appearance once in a while, he genuinely enjoyed the winter activities. As a rule.

But the rules had stopped applying, the moment Claire had arrived. With her, he felt more like a novice than a pro, in charge neither of himself nor those around him. She made the ordinary seem complicated which, for a straightforward man like himself, was an irritation he didn't need.

She meddled, and when he called her on it, as he had that morning on the chairlift, her big gray eyes brimmed with such hurt reproach that he wanted to crawl under a rock for being such a jerk. And it was precisely that—her ability to undermine him, to leave him teetering on the edge of an emotional abyss the likes of which he hadn't known since the months immediately after Jenny's death, that disturbed him the most.

He didn't want to examine too closely why that was so. It was easier to write the whole matter off as the price of doing business. Occasionally, a guest was difficult; this week—Christmas week, when he least needed it—her name happened to be Claire Durocher.

What wasn't so easy to dismiss, though, was his entirely visceral reaction to the sight of her skating with Eric. He was on his way back to the house to shower and change into his dinner suit for the formal evening ahead when he happened to notice them gliding in perfect tandem over the ice. Eric had his arm firmly around her waist and she was gazing up at him the way women frequently did, as if they'd suddenly been presented with the gift-wrapped answer to all their romantic dreams. He heard her laughter carrying clearly in the still air, saw her reach behind her back to catch at his hand.

As he had all too often in recent days, Zach found himself pausing in the lee of a pine where he could watch unobserved. The sun had dipped below the ridge to the west, leaving behind nothing but a faint orange reflection on the frozen surface of the lake. Already the shadows beneath the tree were deep and concealing.

He told himself he was merely doing what he did best: observing to make sure that guests were getting their money's worth. Most of them were skating in a rough circle near the shore. All except Eric, who was whirling Claire farther out on the ice—and Mel, who'd been left by herself to twiddle her thumbs or try to strike up an acquaintance with strangers. The jerk! Didn't the man know how much his visits meant to the kid? As for Claire, her professed concern for Mel hadn't lasted long. She'd ditched her the minute a more likely prospect had shown up.

Stepping out from under the tree, Zach made his way toward where his daughter stood like an abandoned waif watching the two figures far out on the ice. His heart ached for her. She looked so alone, so...uncared-for.

"Hey, kiddo," he said, joining her on the lakeshore and slinging an arm around her shoulders. "How come you're not out there showing the rest how it's done?"

She shrugged, as much, he suspected, to try to dislodge his arm as to indicate her mood. "It's boring doing the same old stuff all the time."

Boring. It was a word he heard from her a lot these days. "Since when did Christmas become boring, Mel?"

She rolled her eyes. "It's not just Christmas, it's this place, Dad. Why can't you just let me go to boarding school?"

"Because I'd miss you."

"Yeah, right! Like you're always there when I need you!"

Oh, brother! Did all kids know just where to stick the knife to make it hurt the most, or was it his daughter's particular talent? "I try to be, Mel, but just lately you haven't seemed particularly interested in doing things with me. Just this morning when I suggested we ski the back run together, you insisted on having Claire come along, too."

At the mention of Claire's name, Mel tried and didn't quite succeed in stifling a sob. It bubbled out in a little moan.

But she's grown tired of you already, baby, and found a new toy to play with....

He couldn't stand watching his child's pain as her eyes tracked Claire and Eric.

"Listen," he said, steering her up the bank toward home. "Uncle Eric's not the only one who enjoys having a pretty girl on his arm. How'd you like to be your old man's date at dinner tonight? Roberto's putting on quite a spread to kick off the official Christmas program."

"You don't want some dumb ugly kid like me hanging around," she hiccupped.

"You're not some dumb ugly kid. You're my beautiful daughter."

"Even if that was true, I couldn't go." She pulled away from him and tugged the hem of his old sweater until it stretched past her knees. "I don't have anything to wear."

May God forgive him, he laughed in the face of this latest tragedy. "Women say that all the time, but they somehow manage to dress to the nines anyway. Tell you what: you go jump in the shower and I'll figure something out."

"Like what? Dad, you know you don't know anything about women's clothes. You don't even know anything about *women*!"

"Thanks for the vote of confidence, kiddo!" He gave her a pat on the backside. "Go scrub off some of that grime and leave the rest to me. You might not believe I'm Santa Claus anymore but I've still got a few tricks up my sleeve and I guarantee you'll look like a million dollars by this evening."

When she hesitated and looked back at him doubtfully, he held her gaze and hoped he'd be able to carry through on his promise. Because she was right: when it came to women, he was badly out of practice. But if he had to hogtie her to get her to cooperate, he was, just this once, going to actively enlist Claire Durocher's help.

He showed up at the lake again just as they came off the ice. Eric flung himself down on a bench and looked around. "Hey, where's the kid?"

"If you're referring to Melanie," Zach said, keeping his anger on as tight a leash as he could muster, "she's gone home."

"What for? We told her we wouldn't be long and to wait for us."

"Maybe she found something more interesting to do than hanging around in the cold waiting for people who didn't seem particularly anxious for her company."

The self-involved jackass didn't pick up on the fact that the chill in the air wasn't entirely due to the weather, but

Claire noticed. She'd been bent over, untying her skates, but Zach's remark hit home. At his words she lifted her head and flung a sidelong glance his way.

Still oblivious, Eric slid guards over his own skates and said, "It's cold enough, all right. Anybody interested in joining me in the bar for hot buttered rum?"

Zach knew the invitation was intended for Claire but he didn't give her a chance to reply. "Count us out," he said shortly, grasping her arm. "We've got other plans."

She raised her eyebrows questioningly but didn't say a word as he towed her up the bank. Only when they were out of earshot of the crowd did she break the silence. "You've got a problem with Melanie?"

"No," he said. "You have."

"*Me?* Why, what have I done?"

"Besides leaving her to freeze while you make cozy with her uncle, you mean?"

"But that's not what happened! She said she'd rather watch than skate."

"Because, to quote you, she felt like a third wheel."

The soulful gray eyes did a number on him again. "Ah, *non!*"

"Ah, *oui!*" he sneered. "She might be only thirteen, but she's no fool. She knows when she's not really wanted."

"That's not fair, and you know it," she protested.

"All I know is that right now she's bawling her eyes out because her so-called friend has dumped her and worse, taken her uncle away from her, too, though why she thinks he hung the moon, I'll never understand."

"What do you mean, 'hung the moon'?"

"She idolizes him. He can do no wrong in her eyes." He stopped and shook his head, exasperated. "Never mind! What I'm trying to say is, unless all your talk of being her friend is just so much hot air, now's the time for you to put your money where your mouth is and prove it."

"I must put hot money in my mouth?"

"Oh, for Pete's sake!" They were almost at the house and he still hadn't made his point. "Look, Mel's miserable. Her confidence is at an all-time low. She thinks she's ugly and stupid, and I don't seem able to change her mind. So I'm asking you to see what you can do."

"You want me to…interfere?"

"Yes," he spat out, unreasonably furious with her for making him come out and say it. "I'm giving you permission to interfere, just this once."

She could have enjoyed his discomfiture. Made him grovel. Given his reaction to her, he probably would have, if he'd been in her place. But to her credit, she forfeited that pleasure and cut to the chase. "What do you want me to do?"

"I've told her she can join us for dinner in the lodge tonight and I think she'd like to come but she's dragging her feet because she's got nothing to wear."

"Does she really have nothing?"

"Nothing fancy, no." He scratched his head, trying to remember when he'd last seen Mel dressed up. "I guess the only party clothes she's got are those her mother bought. I don't suppose any of them fit her any more."

Claire's expression didn't change, but her unblinking stare spoke volumes of accusation. *What kind of father are you that you haven't bothered to make sure your child owns a decent party dress?* "I don't suppose they do," she said at last.

He squirmed. "Okay, I get the message: you can't make a silk purse out of a sow's ear. Sorry I even asked. Mel probably doesn't really want to attend the dinner anyway."

"Be quiet!" she scolded. "How can you call your daughter a pig?"

"I didn't. I meant you can't be expected to work miracles. Godmothers with magic wands don't exist outside of fairy tales."

"But I'm a mistress of illusion, Zachary, didn't you know that? And it'll be my pleasure to transform her."

He wasn't sure he understood what the reference to illusion meant, nor did he care to find out. It was the part that came after that counted. "Are you saying you'll help?"

She smiled and he wished he could look away. She had a smile that put the sun and the stars to shame. It illuminated everything it touched, including him. It made right now more bearable, and gave hope to tomorrow. It made him believe in dreams he thought he'd outgrown a long time ago. "It will be my pleasure to...interfere."

"Then I'll make myself scarce for half an hour. Will that be time enough?"

The smile blossomed into a laugh. "*Non*. But don't let that keep you away because we'll work the miracles *chez moi*."

"Thanks." He caught her hand in his, then hastily dropped it again. Touching her was not a good idea. He'd learned that the night she arrived, and again this morning, on the chairlift. But the vivacity in her lovely heart-shaped face tempted him, made him want to take risks he'd normally avoid. He cleared his throat. "I owe you one."

"You owe me nothing," she said, the laughter fading and leaving her mouth soft and somehow sad. "But perhaps, if you're pleased with how Melanie looks tonight, you'll forget that I was an ache in the neck when I first arrived here and we can turn to an empty page."

"You're mangling the language again, but I get your drift."

"Drift?" She looked dubiously at the snow piled up beside the path.

"Let me rephrase that," he said, unable to control the grin spreading over his face. "I understand what you mean, and it's a deal. Make my little Cinderella feel special, just for tonight—you know what I mean—" *The way you look special.* It was what he wanted to say, but he couldn't bring himself to speak the words, they gave away too much of what he was feeling. He cleared his throat. "Do that, and we'll wipe the slate clean and start over."

She looked at him so long and with such comprehension that he felt himself flushing. With unerring instinct, she'd read his thoughts exactly. When she replied, her voice, always beguiling with its husky foreign intonation, captivated him in a new and different way. "If you mean what I think you mean, then I'm flattered, Zachary."

For one absurd moment, a sort of dizziness swept over him and he found himself swaying dangerously close to that lovely face, to that mouth. Trapped in the fascination of the sight and sound of her, he teetered, rocking on the balls of his feet and reaching blindly at nothing with his hands.

And then common sense returned, edged with panic. Hadn't she just admitted she was the mistress of illusion, as insubstantial as a dream? He meant nothing to her and she meant nothing to him. Nothing! She was the last woman in the world he could afford to get involved with. "It's not a done deal yet," he said brusquely, turning away. "You've still to fulfill your part of the bargain."

Claire flung open the doors of the closet in the dressing room, surveyed the contents and sighed. She had so many things in her Paris apartment that would have been perfect for Melanie, if only she'd known.

But, *Make my little Cinderella special just for tonight,* he had said, his eyes tracking her body as intimately as a lover's, and she would move heaven and earth rather than let him down. Sliding the padded hangers back and forth, she made her selections, then quickly stripped off her own clothes and stepped into the shower.

She was smoothing sheer silk stockings up her legs when Zachary phoned. "I want to get to the lodge early to receive everybody. Are you about ready to leave?"

Mon dieu! She had yet to dry her hair, let alone apply a little makeup. As for Melanie, she still lay on the couch in the salon, with cotton pads soaked in ice water over her eyes to reduce the redness from her tears, and her fingers fanned apart as the pale rose polish dried on her nails.

"Not quite, Zachary," she said, deciding a little white lie was justified. "Why don't you go ahead without us?"

"You sure you don't mind walking over on your own?"

"Not a bit," she said. "Melanie will be fashionably late for her first grown-up evening affair and make a grand entrance."

But everything took longer than Claire had anticipated and they were more than just fashionably late. The gong, booming out its summons to dinner, might as well have been intended to announce their eventual arrival at the cocktail reception in the lounge. All eyes turned their way, some mildly curious, some blankly indifferent—and one pair, Zachary's, blazingly alive with shock.

Magnificent in a well-cut dinner jacket, he was engaged in conversation with a group of guests, but at the sight of his daughter, he stopped in mid-sentence and his jaw dropped.

To Claire, poised on the threshold of the room with

Melanie at her side, the moment seemed to last forever. Fraught with sudden disquieting tension, it stretched and expanded, seeming to smother the lively buzz of conversation to a murmur. She was aware of movement, of people eventually drifting past as they made their way to the dining room, until there were only four of them left: Melanie, herself, the cowboy person, McBride, and Zachary. And still he said nothing.

Melanie shrank against her. "Oh, boy, Claire! Dad doesn't look exactly thrilled to see us."

Claire feared she was right and quailed a little herself. His mouth had snapped shut and he seemed, for once, at a loss for words. But the scowl darkening his expression spoke clearly enough of his displeasure.

Avoiding his eye, she put on her most brilliant smile and addressed not him, but McBride, who sat on a stool at the bar. He had left his tall hat and jeans at home for once and dressed in a dark suit and a white shirt with a black string tie. Although he still wore boots, they were black and highly polished, unlike the work-worn pair he favored during the day. But it was his beaming smile and not his finery which prompted Claire to steer Melanie toward him.

"We've left it a little late to join you for an aperitif, I'm afraid, so would you mind taking Melanie in to dinner?"

"Well, if that don't make this my lucky day!" he exclaimed, sliding to his feet and extending his elbow. "I'd be honored, mamselle. Mel, you're the prettiest darn sight these old eyes of mine have seen in a coon's age. Let's go knock their socks off, darlin'."

She went without a murmur. Considering he was by then livid with anger, Claire supposed it was a tribute to his self-discipline that Zachary waited until they were alone before directing the brunt of his anger where he felt it rightly belonged. On her.

"Do you mind explaining to me," he ground out from between clenched teeth, "what the hell that was that just walked out of here?"

CHAPTER FIVE

BRACING herself, Claire stood her ground and matched him glare for glare. "Surely you mean who? Not that I'm surprised you didn't recognize her! But for your information, that was *la belle Mademoiselle* Alexander, transformed into a beautiful young lady just as you directed."

"If I'd known you'd interpret that to mean I wanted her tarted up to look like something picked off the back streets of the nearest red light district, I'd have asked for help elsewhere."

She gasped in shock. Although he couldn't possibly know it, his remark had struck woundingly close to home. She'd been born in a red light district, had grown up there—aware, humiliated, and helpless to change her circumstances—and no amount of acquired refinement had ever quite erased the shame. But not until he uttered those contemptuous words did she realize how deeply she feared being exposed for the impostor she undoubtedly was.

Dear Lord, how he would despise her, if he knew!

Stalling until she could regain her composure, she turned away from him, poured a glass of sparkling water at the bar, and took a sip. When she was sure her voice wouldn't betray her by breaking, she faced him again. "Although your daughter is undoubtedly a lady, Zachary," she said, countering his rage with hard-won disdain, "you are most certainly no gentleman."

"How I measure up in your eyes isn't the issue, my dear."

My dear, he said, lacing what should have been a term

of affection with outright insult. Regarding him over the rim of her glass, she said, "Then what is?"

"You need to ask?" He flung up his hands. "Mel's only thirteen, for crying out loud! She's got no business being dolled up to look twenty."

"I did the best I could with what I had at hand."

"You went overboard."

"If you consider a taffeta silk skirt and matching cream blouse too extreme a fashion statement," she said, "then perhaps you've been too long in the wilderness, and forgotten that there's another world where something other than dull essentials play a part in a woman's wardrobe." She lowered her lashes and tilted one shoulder in a provocative gesture of contempt. "Or perhaps it's simply a fact you never acknowledged in the first place."

"Your carefully rehearsed feminine wiles are wasted on me," he snapped, the fire in his eyes at once beautiful and terrifying, "so save them for someone more easily impressed. My only interest in you stems from the dismal ideas you're putting in my daughter's head."

"And I strike you as a bad influence? As a woman lacking in good taste or good sense?"

"Lacking in good sense certainly! She's wearing diamonds and reeking of perfume, not to mention tottering around in high heels. And what have you done to her hair?"

"Besides comb out the tangles, you mean?"

He brought his open palm down on the bar with an almighty thud that sent the assorted glassware tinkling like distant bells. "Stop playing games! You know what I'm talking about."

"I curled it a little, then pinned it up to show off her pretty neck."

"I don't care to have my daughter's neck exposed to

public scrutiny—nor any other part of her, come to that! I particularly don't care to have you teaching her things she'd be better off not knowing.''

Moistening her lips with another sip of water, Claire perched on the nearest stool and crossed her legs so that the slit in the front of her skirt swung open to reveal an inch or two of silk-clad thigh. ''What sort of things, Zachary?'' she inquired, swinging one ankle demurely. ''To enjoy her youth? To take pride in looking and feeling her best? You prefer that she hide herself away in your home, unhappy and lonely?''

''She's not unhappy.''

''You told me yourself, just this afternoon, that she is, but I'm beginning to think you don't know your daughter well enough to recognize what it is she really feels or needs.''

''And I suppose you do?''

''It isn't very difficult to determine.''

''Oh? You have a degree in adolescent psychology, do you?''

''No.''

He laughed scornfully. ''Then forgive me if I dismiss you and your opinions as irrelevant.''

''I don't need to be a psychologist to understand Melanie, *mon ami*, because despite the difference in our ages, under the skin we're the same: both women who need and deserve to feel alive and of importance to someone.''

''Again, I must disagree. She is a child and you...'' As though drawn by a magnet, his gaze traveled the length of her, dwelling a long moment on her face, and at the point where her skirt fell open above her knee, then sliding to the ankle she continued to swing negligently even though the coward in her longed to run away and hide.

He swallowed and, like a sword left too long out in the

rain, his voice lost its steely edge and emerged hoarse with rust. "You are…wrong if you think she's not important to me. I would lay down my life for her."

"Of course you would, because you love her. But to a child, a parent's love is…" She groped her hand in the air, searching to express herself in a way that would have meaning for the man standing so tall and troubled before her. "It is an obligation. She needs to feel the warmth of others if she is to thrive, to know joie de vivre. We all do, Zachary. Otherwise, we're like flowers without water. We dry up and we die inside until all that's left is a shell that crumbles at a touch."

She had not, after all, found the right words. Flowers, shells—they weren't part of his frozen world. He didn't understand. Recovering from his brief show of emotion, he schooled his features into an expressionless mask and waited for her to make a point which had some meaning.

"Well," she said regretfully, slipping off the stool and smoothing her dress over her hips, "I can see you're unmoved by my efforts to make you take a wider view, so I'll seek out the company of those who don't find me quite so tiresome. The meal your chef has prepared smells divine and leaves me anxious to sample dinner. *Bon appetit,* Zachary!"

It wasn't easy to make a dignified exit, not when every instinct she possessed urged her to scurry away like a deranged mouse, but she managed it, even though the effort cost her dearly.

He didn't want to look at her, but damn it, he couldn't help himself. She walked the way she skied, with a supple, effortless grace that drew the eye. Unwillingly, he watched, admiring her regal posture, the sheer bloody elegance of her. And knew he'd condemned her unfairly when he'd accused her of lacking good taste. The woman exuded style and class from the tips of her toes to the top of her exquisitely coiffed head.

Still… He scratched his jaw irritably, unable to reconcile the Mel he knew with the coltish young stranger who'd paraded into the lounge with diamonds strung through her hair and lipstick on her mouth. Okay, so the lipstick was pale pink, barely more than a blush of color, and the flush on her cheeks had probably been natural, and maybe all kids her age liked to dabble with makeup—but diamonds? Uh-uh! That was too over the top for his peace of mind.

On the other hand, maybe Claire had hit closer to the truth than he cared to admit, because he couldn't remember when he'd last seen his daughter looking so radiant. Talk about lighting up the room the minute she walked in—until she'd seen his scowl, that was!

He downed what was left of his drink and grimaced. The ice had long since melted in the glass, diluting the Scotch to little more than tepid mouthwash. In light of the evening ahead, he could have used a belt of something with more kick but things were off to a bad enough start, without his adding alcohol to the mix.

For Mel's sake, he'd arranged for Claire to sit at his table—an ill-conceived decision, given the woman's ability to get under his skin in less time than it took to swat a fly. Maybe the feeling was mutual and she'd have had the good sense to find a seat somewhere else.

The hope, faint at best, was dashed the minute he strode into the dining room. She was at her appointed place, with Eric on her left, though if he inched much closer, he'd be in her lap. And Mel, looking dauntingly grown-up, sat sandwiched between Eric and McBride.

Zach pulled out his own chair on the opposite side of

the table and nodded to the company at large. "Sorry if I kept you all waiting."

Eric leered at Claire, the glitter in his eye and the way he was practically drooling on her neck indication enough that he was already half-cut. "That's okay, buddy. We managed to keep ourselves entertained."

"No doubt," Zach said shortly, reminding himself that Eric was his late wife's brother and his daughter's uncle. With his own parents retired in Arizona and his sister living in New Zealand, he had to guard against showing his contempt for the man. Family members were in too short supply.

Instead, he looked around at the well-dressed crowd who'd be sharing this Christmas at Topaz Lake. Filled to capacity except for the four places reserved for the family scheduled to arrive the next morning, the dining room buzzed with animated conversation. The combination of superb wines, food and service, along with the smell of freshly cut evergreens and the twinkle of lights on the tree made for an atmosphere filled with seasonal goodwill.

Almost guiltily, he brought his gaze to rest again on Mel. She was glowing, no doubt about it, and he supposed that, to be fair, he *did* have Claire to thank for that. As for Claire herself... Zach looked away again quickly, before he was caught staring.

How did she manage to create such an effect with so little? Her dress was navy blue and simple to the point of plain, a statement in itself beside the rich winter velvets and brocades worn by the other women. Long sleeved, with a scooped neckline and that teasing slit up the front of the skirt now safely hidden beneath the table, it sort of slithered over her curves like liquid satin.

It must be the jewelry that made it so eye-catching; diamonds again, swinging from her ears, nesting on the rich fabric just about where her cleavage began, and sparkling on her hand and wrist. Considering the number she'd also managed to plaster on Mel, she must have packed along half a suitcase of the things, in addition to all the designer clothes she'd also brought.

Not that she was alone in her extravagance, he had to admit. The woman to his left had a pigeon's blood ruby the size of an egg hanging around her neck, while another to his right fairly dazzled the eye with her emeralds.

He'd never been able to afford such luxury for Jenny. The best he'd been able to offer had been the pearls he'd given her for their wedding anniversary, the year before she died. After the funeral, he'd put them in the office safe, intending to keep them for Mel when she was old enough to wear them and never dreaming that he'd be upstaged by a woman with a taste for diamonds that must keep De Beers laughing twelve months a year.

Too caught up in his own brooding to care about much else, he slouched in his seat as the main course was cleared away, content to be a spectator at his own party. The tables were arranged in a circle, leaving the middle of the floor empty. While some guests lingered over coffee and dessert, others chose to liven up the proceedings with dancing. Eric was among the first, parading Claire into the thick of things as if she were a trophy he'd won.

Not to be outdone, McBride coaxed Mel onto the floor. Blushing and giggling, she allowed him to swing her around in something between a polka and a trot, a move executed with more energy than style. Not that she seemed to mind.

"A child needs to feel the warmth of others, to know joie de vivre," Claire had said, and Zach had the uncomfortable feeling she might have been right. It was more than the diamonds that were making Mel sparkle.

The booze, meanwhile, was taking its usual toll on Eric. He had his arm wrapped so far around Claire's waist that it practically met itself coming back. In typical fashion, when she tried to put a little distance between herself and her partner, he made the most of opportunity and let his sweaty hand slip dangerously close to cupping her behind.

It wasn't the first time Eric had allowed his baser instincts to get the better of him when he was under the influence of alcohol, but it was the first time Zach experienced quite such a violent reaction to the spectacle. A sort of red film clouded his consciousness, dimming his awareness of exactly what happened next. One minute, he was leaning back in his seat, surveying the scene with a certain grim satisfaction, and the next he was on his feet and his chair had gone crashing over.

As though on cue, the music stopped. A log spat furiously in the hearth. Faces turned his way, curious, alarmed, amused. Too late he realized the sight he presented: face flushed, fists clenched, and a muscle in his cheek twitching repeatedly despite his clamping his teeth together so rigidly it was a wonder he didn't do serious damage to his dental work.

His headwaiter approached and asked in an undertone, "Everything okay, boss?"

"Fine," he managed, just about choking on his rage. "Just fine."

She'd come back to the table and slipped into her chair with only a passing glance his way. But he saw the faint lift of her brows, the subtly apologetic tilt of one shoulder, as though she were saying, "Don't blame me for what you saw. I didn't ask to be pawed like that."

But Eric, who wasn't so far gone that he didn't know when to draw in his horns, avoided his eye altogether and made a big production of talking to Mel, who lapped up the attention.

Typical, to hide behind a defenseless child! Zach thought, itching to pick up his brother-in-law by the scruff of the neck and turf him out into the snow. But he'd made fool enough of himself already, and Eric wasn't worth an encore.

Shooting his cuffs into place and shrugging his jacket more comfortably over his shoulders, he instead picked up the fallen chair and, aware that he was still the object of some curiosity by the rest of his party, approached Claire and said, "Would you care to dance?"

She looked at him as if he'd gone mad, her gray eyes wide and incredulous, then peered into her wine as if she thought he might be planning to spike it with ground glass when her back was turned. "You want to dance with me?"

Don't make me regret asking, he thought savagely, but the annoyance faded into something warm and lovely around his heart when, at his nod, she rose to her feet in a rustle of midnight blue silk and placed her hand in his.

Cautiously, he drew her into his arms—cautious because he didn't know how to interpret the feelings she brought to the fore in him. She was just a woman, pretty enough but not dramatically beautiful, except perhaps for her big eyes and long black lashes, so silky they gleamed against her cheek; and for her porcelain-fine skin, and the thick dark hair piled just high enough that it touched his chin as they danced. And her heart-shaped face and lush mouth. Except for those things and a slender body, she was…

He inhaled, capturing the scent of her hair. Slid his arm more firmly around that narrow waist and felt the pressure of her breasts against his chest. Caught his hand wanting to trespass, and the weight of desire tugging at him. She was lovely, damn it, and he was no better than Eric!

Thrusting her a decent distance away, he searched for something brilliant and witty to say. The best he could come up with was, "You're very quiet."

"I'm very surprised, Zachary."

"Why?"

"Because you asked me to dance. I thought you were angry with me."

"Not with you," he said, pulling her a little closer again because looking into her eyes at such close quarters left him feeling as if he'd been poleaxed. "With my brother-in-law. He gets a little…carried away sometimes, but that's no excuse for the kind of liberties he was taking with you—unless you invited them, of course."

"I certainly did not," she said, fitting herself against him in a way which refuted her claim because, if she'd snugged up to Eric the way she was cuddling up to him, it was no wonder the poor slob had been all hands, drunk or sober. "Nor was I referring to that when I said I thought you were angry with me. I was referring to Melanie."

May-lah-nee, she said, managing to embroider the name with enchantment.

"I had hoped you would be pleased with how I made her look, Zachary."

Zach-arree. More enchantment, uttered low and this time taking direct aim at a susceptibility in himself he neither welcomed nor trusted. He was in trouble up to his armpits if he let himself be seduced by the way a woman spoke his name!

"I am pleased," he said, and looked around surprised, as if he thought someone else had spoken, because that wasn't what he'd intended to say at all. But instead of rectifying the error, he compounded it. "And if I seemed ungrateful for the trouble you've taken, I apologize. It's just that I was a bit stunned at the transformation. I hadn't realized that Mel had grown so pretty.''

"Sometimes," she said, "physical changes can happen quickly and take a person off guard.''

No kidding! He'd been caught so off guard that, if she suddenly moved away, he stood to be publicly embarrassed at the physical change she'd brought about in him!

He swallowed and attempted to push aside the thoughts crowding his mind, of things he'd like to do with this woman. It didn't help any to have Karen Carpenter's voice haunting the room with "Merry Christmas, Darling," or for one of the waiters to choose that moment to dim all the lights except for those on the tree, leaving the room full of flickering shadows and himself awash in sudden aching nostalgia.

He was missing Jenny, that was all. It happened every year at this time, striking without warning, a swift, sharp stab of regret for the loss her death had brought: Mel without a mother, the house lacking a woman's caring touch, and himself alone every night in a bed meant to hold two.

"How come you're here by yourself?" he asked abruptly, leaning back to look down at Claire's upturned face. Then, realizing she might interpret the question as a come-on, hurried to add, "I mean, everyone else is with someone and it's Christmas, and—''

"I know what you mean," she said. "You wonder if I'm lonely and the answer is yes, of course I am, especially at Christmas. And a little all year long, as well, because, in the best of all worlds, I believe God intended a woman to find a man to be her soul mate. But...'' She gave one of her little shrugs and tilted her head to one side. "I'd rather be alone than clinging to someone I don't love and who can't love me. I've seen too often how painful such alliances can be.''

Her candor, untouched as it was by self-pity, disarmed him and left him altogether too susceptible to her. "Were your parents happily married, Claire?"

She stiffened and drew away from him. "No," she said, with a finality that completely stifled the tentative intimacy they'd established.

Just as well, he reasoned. He was no monk. He had urges just like any other man and sometimes he indulged them— but discreetly and never with resort guests. There was a woman in Broome—Elaine, the local nurse. He'd met her when he'd taken one of his staff to the clinic with a separated shoulder. A nice woman, unmarried, uncomplicated, undemanding. Warm and welcoming, but accepting that his time with her was limited to a few hours. There'd never been any question of their getting married, nor would there ever be. Because, in his heart, he was still married to Jenny.

He'd do well to remember that. Harboring sexual fantasies about the woman temporarily living next door had more to do with proximity than attraction. That summed the whole matter up in a nutshell.

"Not only am I neglecting my other guests, I'm also monopolizing you when I know every other man in the room would give his eyeteeth to dance with you," he said, steering her to the edge of the floor and depositing her near their table before all his fine logic went up in smoke. "Please forgive me."

Perplexed, she stared after him as he strode across the room. What an unpredictable man he was, so agreeable one moment, so aloof the next. He didn't want to be close, not emotionally and not physically, that was the thing. He held himself at a distance always, even when he was being charming.

Briefly, he'd seemed to teeter on the edge of a certain

hunger and she'd thought that, if they'd been alone, he might have given in to desire and kissed her. But the moment passed so swiftly that she couldn't be sure and watching him now, as he circled the floor with another woman in his arms, she thought she surely must have imagined his momentary lapse.

From the corner of her eye she saw the brother-in-law weaving his way toward her, leaving Melanie alone at the table and looking soulful as a little lost dog. Sidestepping his obvious intention to ask her to dance again, Claire slipped into the empty seat next to her. "You look tired, Melanie, and I'm feeling a little like that myself. How would you like to sneak away from here and watch a Christmas video at my place?"

Overhearing, Eric said, "Sounds like a fine idea to me. Okay if I join you?"

In fact, it wasn't, not entirely. Claire suspected he'd drunk a little too much wine with dinner. But Melanie's face had lit up with pleasure at the suggestion and she hadn't the heart to disappoint her. "If you like."

Within minutes they were outside, where a million stars spangled the sky and a round white moon turned the frozen lake to a sheet of silver. Grabbing them each by the hand, Eric broke into a run and towed them boisterously behind him, sending their long skirts flapping around their ankles. They slipped and slithered along the path, and ended up laughing breathlessly at the foot of the steps leading to Zachary's house.

"Gee, Claire, I got snow on your outfit," Melanie gasped, brushing at the flakes clinging to the hem of her skirt.

"It won't hurt, *chérie*, but you'd be wise to change into something dry before you catch cold." Claire shooed her toward her side of the building. "Put on your pajamas and robe, and I'll leave my door unlocked so that you can let yourself in when you're ready."

"Good idea!" Eric rubbed his gloved hands together. "While you're doing that, Mel, I'll get the fire going and bribe Claire to make us some hot chocolate."

Grabbing an armload of logs from the bin at the end of the veranda, he followed Claire into the house and while she hung up her coat and removed her boots, he stirred the fire to life in the salon. That done, he came to lean on the breakfast bar and watched as she prepared the hot chocolate.

"Not many women would give up a fancy party just to keep a kid entertained," he said, his voice as caressing as his gaze. "In my book that makes you a pretty special lady, Claire Durocher."

"On the contrary," she replied, determined not to acknowledge the air of intimacy he was trying to establish. "If anything, I'm being selfish. I enjoy Melanie's company."

"So much that you're prepared to waste a heaven-sent opportunity for us to get to know each other better?" He leaned close enough that his wine-flavored breath fanned her face.

She pulled back and continued spooning chocolate flakes into a thermos jug. "If you're suggesting that I tell Melanie I've changed my mind and no longer wish to watch television with her—"

"Well, it did occur to me we could cut the evening short and send her packing off to her own little bed before too long. But if you're determined to stick to the original plan, I'd better make the most of the moment at hand."

So suddenly that she was caught off guard, he leaned across the counter again and, grasping her by the shoulders, tugged her close enough to plant his mouth on hers.

Momentarily too surprised to resist, she endured the embrace, but when he showed no sign of ending the kiss, she fixed him in a wide-open gaze and left her lips firmly closed despite his efforts to persuade her otherwise. Over the sound of the electric kettle gurgling at her elbow and the carols playing softly on the stereo, she thought she heard Melanie at the front door and offered up a silent prayer of thanks. One way or another, his attempts at seduction would be short-lived.

But no one came into view and since he clearly interpreted her response as passive acceptance of his advances, Claire knew she must rebuff him more forcefully. Placing both hands flat on his chest, she shoved him off. "Please don't do that again, Eric."

He stared at her, looking somewhat like a fish gasping for air. "Why not?"

His voice was a little slurred and his face unhealthily flushed. Realizing too late that the fresh night air had not sobered him up, she sighed. Trying to reason with a drunk was, at best, difficult. "Because I don't want you to," she told him firmly.

"It was only a kiss," he said, sidling around the bar.

Seeing that she would find herself trapped if she remained where she was, she quickly moved into the open area of the room. "Oh, come now, Eric, let's be honest. You were hoping it would be the prelude to something more."

"Can you blame me?" he said amiably, following her and flinging an arm around her shoulder.

He was in worse shape than she'd thought, and no fit sight for an impressionable teenager. Staggering slightly beneath his weight, she steered him out into the hall, anxious to be rid of him before Melanie appeared.

He accompanied her willingly enough but when she tried

to make for the front door, he opted for the narrower corridor leading to the bedroom, and it became a battle of wills as to which direction they should follow.

"Oh, no! This way, my friend!" she said, endeavoring to pilot him toward the exit.

But he was not disposed to cooperate and there followed a somewhat undignified struggle in the middle of which the front door burst open. But the measured tread that followed was not that of an exuberant teenager. Rather, it belonged to a man on a mission and it came as no surprise to Claire when Zachary appeared in her line of vision, her taffeta skirt and blouse slung over one arm.

Beseeching him with her eyes, she let out a whimper of distress, a plea he chose to ignore. "Please don't stop on my account," he said, the look on his face suggesting he beheld an indecency beyond words. "I just came to return your things. Mel won't be needing them—or you—again."

CHAPTER SIX

AT THE sound of his brother-in-law's voice, Eric practically fell over. Seizing the moment, Claire pushed him away and followed Zachary into the living room.

Ignoring her, he dumped the clothes on the nearest chair, dropped the sandals on top, then fished from his pocket the necklace she'd woven through Melanie's hair and added it to the heap. That done, he wiped one palm against the other, as if what he'd touched was unclean, spared her one last, scathing glance, and turned to leave. His every gesture spelled such disgust that one might have thought he'd walked in to find her romping naked with Eric, instead of trying to throw him out of her suite.

Of greater concern just then, however, was the reason for Zachary having shown up at all, when the person she'd been expecting for the last ten minutes or more was his daughter. "Just a minute," she said, attempting to detain him as he passed her on his way back to the front door. "Where's Melanie?"

"Not here, thank God!" he replied, shrugging her off with a flick of his wrist.

"But we were going to watch a movie together."

"She changed her mind, and just as well. You've educated her enough for one night. What I just walked in on is one lesson she can do without."

Outraged, Claire exclaimed, "How like you to assume the worst, Zachary! All you saw was—"

"Oh, please, spare me the details!" he cut in with heavy

sarcasm. "Frankly, I'm not sure I could stomach hearing them."

Until that moment, Claire's one thought had been to enlist his help in getting rid of Eric. But his stubborn refusal to give her a fair hearing, or to consider that she might be more sinned against than sinning, had pride joining forces with annoyance. She was tired of trying—and failing—to redeem herself in his eyes. Let him think whatever he pleased! "That's good, Zachary," she retorted. "Because, frankly, what I do and who I choose to do it with is none of your concern."

"It is if it involves my daughter and, by your own admission, you were expecting her to be the one to walk through your front door, not me."

"So?"

"So it happens that she did just that. But you were too busy planning how soon you could get rid of her to notice."

"She was here?" She stared at him, appalled.

"Yes, she was 'ere, Claire," he said, mimicking her accent by dropping the h, "but she's aware enough to know when she's not wanted so she disappeared as quietly as she arrived, loath to break up the cozy little scene she walked in on."

Apparently deciding he'd been excluded from the conversation long enough, Eric came weaving into the room and, regrettably, chose to add his views to the whole sorry business. "You're working up quite a head of steam over nothing, big guy."

Claire closed her eyes and winced as Zachary roared, "Shut up, you drunken oaf! When I want your opinion, I'll ask for it."

"I'm only trying to help."

"You always are, once you've screwed up."

Eric smiled weakly. "What else do you want me to say? I'm sorry if Mel misunderstood what she heard."

"She understood only too well," Zachary snapped, thrusting by them and marching down the hall. "You couldn't wait to be rid of her and, given your reasons, I'm just as glad. But you could've found a more humane way to get your message across."

"How she must be hurting," Claire exclaimed, trailing after him.

She'd have been wiser to keep quiet. Intimidating and rather magnificent in his anger, he turned on her. "As if you'd know!"

"And what makes you think I don't?" she cried, stung by yet another blast of withering contempt.

He wrenched open the front door. "A woman like you on the receiving end of rejection? When hell freezes over!" he sneered, before storming out.

The silence he left behind rang with unspoken censure and dismay. Finally, Eric cleared his throat and said, "I guess you'd like me to leave, too?"

"Indeed yes."

"It's a bit late to say I'm sorry, I know."

Claire sighed. "Melanie's the one deserving an apology, Eric."

"Maybe so, but it'll have to wait. I'm not about to confront Zach Take-No-Prisoners Alexander again tonight."

Small wonder the two men didn't get along, Claire thought, watching him trudge back to the lodge. Eric was spineless, whereas Zachary was made of steel. Strong, tough, decisive, he was quick to defend those he loved, and slow to forgive anyone who hurt them. Melanie was lucky to have him for a father.

But recognizing that didn't relieve Claire of her next move. She couldn't put off until tomorrow something that needed to be remedied tonight. Reaching for her cape, she drew it around her shoulders, slipped on her boots, and went next door.

She had to knock twice before Zachary answered. "What is it now?" he growled. "The bed not big enough for your sexual acrobatics?"

"I'd like to speak to Melanie," she said quietly.

"Absolutely not. She's heard enough for one night."

"Zachary, please! She really did misunderstand the situation and if she'd waited a little longer, she'd have realized that."

"You mean, 'Let's get rid of the brat so that we can play mattress tag' is open to more than one interpretation? I don't think so!" He laughed scornfully and craned his neck to look over her shoulder. "Where is lover boy, by the way? Hiding behind your skirt?"

"He's gone back to the lodge."

"Aw, shucks! Did I chase him off?"

"No, I did."

"Seems no one had a good time tonight, then, doesn't it?"

"Sadly, not. But whatever else you think me capable of, you must know that I'd never intentionally hurt Melanie's feelings."

"Intentional or not, I know she's in tears for the second time today because of you."

"All the more reason, then, for me to be the one to put matters right." Shivering, Claire pulled the cape more tightly around her. "Won't you please let me come in and speak to her, just for a moment? I'd like to make amends, if I can."

"It's okay, Dad," a small voice said from somewhere behind him. "I don't mind talking to her."

He glanced over his shoulder at the figure half-hidden

by the shadows at the end of the big entrance hall. "You
sure you're up for this, Mel? Because if you're not, you
don't have to go through with it."

"I'm sure."

With marked reluctance, he stepped back to allow Claire
entry, but caught her elbow just as she passed him and
muttered grimly, "You've got five minutes, and you'd better not put a foot wrong, lady, or I'll have you out of here
so fast, you'll bounce!"

Not deigning to dignify such a threat with a response,
she stalked past him to Melanie and swept her up in a hug.
"Oh, *chérie*," she whispered, "I never meant for your special evening to end like this."

"It's okay," the child said again, but it wasn't. Her voice
quivered like a leaf in a storm.

Stepping back slightly, Claire cupped the little face between her hands, guilt-stricken by the red-rimmed eyes and
trembling mouth confronting her. "It's never okay for one
person to make another feel unwanted, even by accident.
Will you let me try to explain what really happened?"

Melanie shrugged. "Okay. We can go to my room, if
you like."

Looming on the threshold like an avenging angel, her
father said, "Why can't you say what has to be said in the
family room?"

"Because it's private girl talk, Dad!"

"So? I won't listen in." He gestured vaguely at a closed
door to the left of the foyer. "I'll be in the den, catching
up on some paperwork."

Melanie waited until her father disappeared as promised
before she led the way to a comfortably furnished room
separated by a breakfast bar from a large, well-equipped
kitchen. Built-in shelves on each side of the fireplace were
filled with an assortment of books and ornaments: a pewter

vase, a millefiori paperweight, a posy of dried roses in a glass-domed display case. But what held Claire's attention was the framed photograph of a younger, carefree Zachary beside a laughing blond woman, and Melanie at age three or four riding on his shoulders against a backdrop of snowy mountain peaks and deep blue sky.

Hastily, Claire looked away, stabbed by a sudden hollow envy. She had never known the sense of family so clearly enjoyed by the three figures in the picture. She had not even one memento of her own childhood that she cherished enough to want to preserve it.

Turning her attention to the matter at hand, she perched on the edge of the nearest couch and patted the cushion beside her in invitation. "Your father's given me only five minutes, Melanie, so let's not waste them."

Warily, the girl joined her. "You don't have to say anything, you know. I watch enough TV to know why Uncle Eric'd want to be alone with you."

"This isn't about what your uncle wants," Claire said, startled by such candor, "but sometimes, when people have been at a party, they become a little…insensitive to the feelings of those around them, and I'm afraid that's what happened with him tonight."

"Oh, you mean he was pickled again? Usually, he sings when he's had too much and Dad bangs on the wall and tells him to put a lid on it."

More taken aback than ever, Claire said, "Well, all I know is that if anyone was in the way tonight, it was your uncle, not you. Do you believe me?"

"I guess." Melanie shrugged. "Sure, if you say so."

"But you don't *sound* sure, so let me add one thing more. You and I haven't known each other very long, but we're friends, yes? And friends don't lie to each other, nor do they break their word. I will always be truthful with you, and I'll try never to break a promise to you.''

''But you're only here for another week, and all the promises in the world don't mean a thing when a person isn't around anymore to keep them,'' the girl said, with a perception beyond her years.

True enough, Claire acknowledged silently, and determined that she'd move heaven and earth before she'd inflict further pain on a child who'd already suffered more grievous loss than anyone her age should have to bear. ''I'm opening a little shop in Vancouver and plan to come back often to make sure it's being well looked after, so you'll see me again. And even when I'm away, there's always the phone. Believe me, Melanie, I treasure our friendship too much to let it end with this holiday.''

''Gee, Claire...!'' The big blue eyes swam with tears. ''Nobody ever said anything like that to me before.''

''Zut!'' Claire exclaimed, close to tears herself. ''If your father finds you crying, he'll carry out this threat and make me bounce, so let me see you smile.''

Melanie scrubbed at her face with a wad of tissue. ''It's okay, I'm not really bawling.''

''But you're exhausted and so am I, and women become emotional at such times. It's been too long a day and we both need our beautiful sleep.''

As quickly as they'd arisen, the tears ceased and Melanie giggled. ''You mean beauty sleep!''

''Never mind. What matters is that we understand each other, the way friends should.'' Claire pressed a kiss on each of her cheeks and prepared to leave. ''So get some sleep now, darling, and I'll see you in the morning.''

''Will you...I mean, would you mind...?''

Hearing the uncertainty in her voice, Claire glanced up from buttoning her cape to find the girl balanced on one foot and rubbing at her instep with the sole of the other foot. "*Oui?* What is it?"

Melanie shrugged awkwardly. "I just wondered if you'd tuck me in before you go."

"Tuck you in?" Claire frowned. "What does that mean?"

"Oh..." As if she'd asked a favor beyond all reason, Melanie stared at her feet. "It means sort of say good-night to me when I'm in bed, but it's okay if you don't want to. I'm way too old for that sort of thing, anyway."

Not want to? Mon dieu, she had spent half a lifetime covering up the pain and damage inflicted by the absence of such parental tenderness in her own life! Barely able to speak for the lump blocking her throat, she murmured, "Oh, *ma petite,* you're never too old! It's every child's birthright to know love."

He was waiting for her when she let herself out of Melanie's room. Bow tie loosened and dangling down the front of his starched dress shirt, he leaned against the wall, one hand in the pocket of his black trousers, the other holding a glass. From the expression on his face, one might have thought he'd caught her pilfering the family silver.

"Before you level any more accusations at me," she began, "Melanie asked me to—"

He swirled the contents of his glass. "I know. I heard."

"You eavesdropped on our conversation?"

"Every word of it," he proclaimed, without a trace of embarrassment.

"You should be ashamed to admit to such a thing!"

Pushing himself away from the wall, he bent down and whispered venomously, "Not half as ashamed as you should be for heaping one lie on top of another."

She stared at him, baffled. "What lies? I spoke only the truth. And why are you whispering?"

He didn't answer immediately. Instead, he grasped her arm and practically frog-marched her back to the family room. Only when the door was securely closed did he say, "Because I don't want Mel overhearing this discussion."

"What's to discuss, Zachary? It seems that no matter how hard I try, I can neither do nor say anything to please you."

"Then maybe you should stop trying so damn hard," he retorted. "Who are you trying to impress anyway, with all this 'friendship' business? We both know that, contrary to your promises, you'll forget Mel the minute you leave here. Do you honestly think you're doing her any favors by pretending otherwise?"

"I am *not* pretending!"

"Oh, give me a break! Rich, single women don't fly halfway around the world to spend Christmas schmoozing with a thirteen-year-old, they come looking for the kind of action my brother-in-law is so eager to supply."

"That might be true of the women you know," she snapped, weary beyond measure by his obdurate refusal to view her motives in any but the worst possible light, "but don't presume to judge me by the same standards. If a man was all I wanted, I could, as you so boorishly imply, have found plenty to accommodate my needs in St. Moritz. Instead, I came here looking for a different kind of satisfaction which I've found in Melanie."

"Too bad," he said flatly. "Because she isn't here to gratify your maternal urges. So go vent your mother-hen frustrations elsewhere and leave my daughter alone."

"Why should I, if I can fill a need in her life that might otherwise go unanswered?"

Her question incensed him. Spinning away from her, he

went to the bar in the corner and splashed more whiskey over the ice cubes in his glass. "Because she already knows what it's like to have a mother, and she isn't looking for a substitute."

"Is that why you're so angry?" Claire exclaimed, with dawning insight. "Are you afraid that, in growing close to me, she'll forget the woman who gave her life? Or that she might need you less?"

He remained with his back to her, his shoulders tense, his stance rigid. "I am afraid of nothing except Mel's being left high and dry when you grow tired of playing guardian angel."

What possessed her then, driving her to put his claim to the test? The arrogant tilt of his head? His absolute certainty that he knew her better than she could ever hope to know herself? Or the photograph on the side table which showed a different Zachary Alexander, one capable of passions other than anger and mistrust?

"You're deceiving yourself, Zachary," she said, coming to stand close behind him. "If that were all that's troubling you, you'd never have asked for my help to begin with. The real truth is, you're afraid of me. I said so once before and now I say so again."

He turned on her, his mouth curled in mocking disbelief. "You annoy the hell out of me, I'll grant you that."

"That, too," she agreed, her voice softly taunting. "And shall I tell you why?"

"I have a feeling you will, whether I want you to, or not."

Daringly, she reached up and stroked her fingertips along the forbidding line of his jaw. "You hide behind Melanie rather than face the fact that you have needs which go beyond merely being a good father. You're a man capable of deep passion, Zachary, something I won't let you forget, and that's why I annoy you, and why you're frightened of me. I threaten your safe, monastic way of life.''

He might have been cast in stone had it not been for the fire in his eyes. For too long, he directed that blazing glare at her, scorching her feature by feature, as if he hoped his doing so would eliminate her from his life, once and for all. Only when it became apparent that she would not conveniently go away did he move, seizing her so abruptly that she would have stumbled had the solid wall of his chest not prevented her.

''Is that a fact?'' he said thickly, and without waiting for an answer, brought his mouth down on hers—not punitively, as she might have expected, given that she'd stirred him to anger yet again, but with an eloquent mastery that left her senses reeling.

Blindly, she clutched at his shoulders for support, digging her fingers into the solid sheath of muscle overlaying bone. She felt the heat of his skin beneath the fabric of his shirt, the strength of his torso imprinted, inch for inch, against hers. She felt the sleek athletic power of him, the legacy of years of rigorous physical activity. But mostly, she felt the passion she'd accused him of, unleashed by degrees in a kiss that devastated her, and she quaked inside.

Almost from the moment she'd met him, she'd wanted to put him to the test, believing she could control the extent of her involvement with him. But in the end, it was her own appetite that betrayed her, inflaming her to a hunger so fierce that she shied way from what it implied. She had started out wanting only his understanding, his acceptance. But suddenly, shockingly, they ceased to be enough. Now, she wanted him, as well.

Sensing her misgivings, he caressed her spine soothingly, as if to say, *Don't be afraid, mon amour.* Splaying his fingers wide, he allowed them to knead a path from the rounded curve of her hips to her shoulder blades and back again.

Lulled by the hypnotic rhythm, she sank against him, allowing him to deepen the kiss, softening and bending before his persuasive finesse and even letting her arms wind trustingly around his neck.

And then, when her defenses were at their weakest, he took advantage of her. Shifting his hands just a fraction, he angled his thumbs to her sides and slid them smoothly past the indentation of her waist and up her ribs to trace a lingering path along the tender side swell of her breasts. The audacity of such a move left her gasping with delicious shock, a response he took as invitation to explore with greater thoroughness the darkest secrets of her mouth.

How was it that the protest she meant to voice emerged as a little moan of pleasure? And when had her eyes fallen closed, drugged by the potency of his kiss? She could not say. All her awareness was centered on the exquisite torture wrought by his clever mouth and hands—until he decided he'd had enough of her, and then all she knew was the desolation of being abandoned by him. Of being flung aside like a toy which had ceased to amuse.

Deprived of the warmth of his mouth on hers, her lips grew cool. Unsupported by his arms, she swayed dizzily. She opened her eyes, searching helplessly to find her bearings, and found herself pinned in the veiled blue gaze of a man whose only emotion might have been that of a collector regarding a not-too-rare butterfly.

She cringed under that scrutiny, aware that to pretend an indifference to him was futile. Her flushed face, her eyelids still heavy with desire, the ragged rhythm of her breathing, and most revealing of all, her nipples straining aggressively against the silk of her dress, they flaunted the truth. Her only consolation lay in the knowledge that, the thoroughness of his inspection notwithstanding, he couldn't possibly detect the flooding heat he'd created between her thighs.

Appalled at being put so thoroughly to rout, she backed away from him, hoping to make contact with a chair, a table—anything against which to regain her balance and a little of her composure. Instead, the back of her knees buckled against the edge of the couch and toppled her in a heap on the cushions.

At that, a hint of derision touched his mouth. "So who's afraid of whom, sweetheart?" he jeered softly, towering over her.

CHAPTER SEVEN

THE next day, the Dawsons and their two children arrived. Because she hadn't slept well the previous night, Claire spent the morning in the beauty spa and so didn't meet them until lunch where she found herself once again assigned to Zachary's table—less, she was sure, because he craved her company than because Melanie had requested it.

The new guests were seated there, also. Shining with healthy good looks, the Dawsons were an attractive family, but it was neither the dentist father, Paul, nor the mother, Linda, smiling graciously over introductions, that painted Melanie's cheeks with excitement.

"Isn't he gorjilious?" she breathed in Claire's ear, referring to the nearly six-foot-tall teenage son, Ian.

Relieved that the unpleasantness of the previous night appeared to have had no lasting effect, Claire laughed. "If you mean, isn't he handsome, then yes, he certainly is."

"You look really nice, too, Claire, the way you've had your hair done and your nails and all. Um…you know that there's a sleigh ride planned for tonight, don't you?"

"I read something about it in the daily bulletin, yes."

Melanie studied a sprig of parsley on her plate as studiously as if it held the key to her future and tried to sound nonchalant. "Do you think you'd have time to do my hair again?"

"Of course, provided your father doesn't mind."

Zachary, whom she'd thought was deep in conversation

with Paul Dawson, suddenly lifted his head and inquired, "What won't her father mind?"

"Nothing, Dad. We were just talking about the sleigh ride tonight and how much fun it'll be. You'll come, won't you, Sue—and you, too, of course, Ian?" The change from tongue-tied adolescent to artfully ingenuous young woman both surprised and amused Claire as Melanie turned first to the Dawsons' daughter, then, as a seeming afterthought, to the son.

The mother noticed, too, and smiled at Claire. "It's nice that they're getting along so well, isn't it? It makes it so much easier for us parents. Your daughter is lovely, by the way."

"Ms. Durocher is not Melanie's mother," Zachary put in, once again seeming to have a third ear tuned in to other people's comments. "She is a guest here, that's all."

Obviously taken aback by such a bald contradiction, Linda flung an apologetic glance at Claire and said, "I'm sorry. She's dark like you and you seem so close that I just assumed—"

"Please don't feel you have to apologize," Claire said, fixing Zachary in a killing glare. "I'm flattered that you thought we were related. If I did have a daughter, I'd want her to be just like Melanie."

"What a lovely thing to say!" Linda tipped her head to one side and regarded Claire curiously. "I thought at first that you're from eastern Canada, but you're not, are you? That accent is distinctly European."

"She's from France," Zachary announced. "And she'll be returning there as soon as the holidays are over."

A flush of annoyance swept over Claire's face. "My English might not be quite as polished as yours, Zachary, but I'm fluent enough to be able to speak for myself most of the time. And it so happens that I'm staying in Canada somewhat longer than you think.''

"Not here at Topaz Valley you aren't,'' he said flatly. "A party from Japan has booked the whole resort for the first two weeks in January and we won't have a closet to spare, let alone the kind of accommodation you demand.''

Satisfied that his snub had hit home, he redirected his attention to his other guests, showering them with the charm he so patently refused to confer on her.

To her horror, Claire found herself on the verge of tears. Why does he go out of his way to humiliate me like this? she wondered miserably. All I've ever wanted is to prove I'm not the shallow, rich shrew he first took me to be, but nothing I say or do seems able to change his mind.

"All you've ever wanted?'' a disparaging little voice inside her echoed. *"For pity's sake, when are you going to stop lying to yourself, Claire? It's not just his mind you want to change, it's his heart, as well. What you really want is for him to love you as you've come to love him.''*

To love him... Mon dieu, it was true!

Dismayed, she toyed with her oysters Florentine and told herself she was a fool to fall in love with a man who patently despised her. Still, the damnable tears persisted until the oysters on her plate blurred into a sea of gray-green and she thought she would choke if she tried to force anything past the lump in her throat. "Please excuse me,'' she murmured, depositing her serviette on the table and pushing back her chair. "I find I'm not very hungry today.''

She reached the foyer just as McBride was coming in. "Everythin' okay, mamselle?'' he asked, holding open the outside door for her. "You seem a mite upset.''

"Just a headache,'' she managed, averting her face and hurrying past him.

Fortunately, she met no one as she rushed along the

lakeshore path and up the steps to Zachary's house. Because McBride's kindly concern had proved her undoing and set the tears to flowing down her face like an early thaw, and she could not have borne for anyone else to witness her distress.

While she'd been out, the housekeeping staff had cleaned her suite and left a fire ready to start in the hearth. Within five minutes, the flames were leaping up the chimney and she was stretched out on the soft leather cushions of the couch, covered by her mohair shawl and with nothing to disturb her peace but the crackle of the burning logs, the occasional swish of snow falling from laden branches outside, and the stereo playing softly in the background.

So why couldn't she drift off into a pleasant afternoon siesta? Why did the Christmas songs all have to do with children and families, reminding her that she'd never known what it was to lean against her mother's knee and experience the joy and wonder of the season? As for Mommy kissing Daddy beneath the mistletoe—oh, not in their house, although Lisette certainly had kissed many other men.

And her daughter's father, what of him? A sailor passing through Marseilles and looking for an evening's entertainment, a married man, a prince, a pauper? Closing her eyes, Claire tried to close out her thoughts as well, knowing the futility of pursuing them. She had inherited his dark hair and gray eyes but beyond that she knew nothing. Who he was, what he was, were secrets her mother had taken to the grave if, indeed, she'd ever known them in the first place.

Be sensible, Claire admonished herself, thinking of the elegance and comfort surrounding her. *Look at how far you've come and stop wishing for more good fortune than you already possess. There was a time when you'd have counted yourself lucky to be the one to scrub the floors in a place like this.*

What was it her mentor, Belle, used to say, on those days when the people didn't come to the street market to hunt for treasures and there was no money for fresh bread or fish? "Even the richest man cannot buy time, my girl. Use today to look and learn. Take the things you value the least and trade them for something of greater worth. Better you hold in your hand one fine piece than horde a boxful of trash."

She'd been talking about paste, of course; jewelry so closely imitating the real thing that it brought a fair price on the secondhand market. But it was a lesson that lent itself to life as well, and Claire had applied it to hers ever since the day she learned how it was that her mother could afford to wear silk stockings when her only child wandered the streets in rags.

Zachary Alexander could belittle her all he liked, but he could never provoke her enough that she'd be willing to sell her self-respect, just to win his favor.

The knowledge comforted her enough that she was able to relax and sleep after all, because when she next became aware of her surroundings, the afternoon had faded into dusk, the fire died to a soft red glow, and Melanie was banging at the door, her eyes filled with the light of first love.

That night, instead of the usual formal meal, dinner was served buffet style. Though still an elegant affair, it left guests free to sit where they chose and in light of her most recent contretemps with Zachary, Claire chose a table as far away from his as possible.

Avoiding him afterward proved just as easy. While he supervised the loading of one sleigh, she joined the group of guests waiting to board the other where McBride was in charge.

As sleighs went, these were really nothing more than buckboards on runners, with a high sprung seat for two at the front. The flat deck behind was filled with bales of straw arranged in a rough pyramid so that people could sit on the lower tier and lean against the higher one at their backs. Though more primitive than what she was used to, each conveyance nevertheless looked quite charming draped in evergreen garlands and pulled by a pair of magnificent black horses.

When it came time for her to board, McBride ran a critical eye over her ivory ski suit and said, "You look too fine to be sitting back there in all that straw, mamselle, so why don't you ride up front with me? We're heading to the fire pit on the other side of the valley and you'll have a better view of where we're going from there."

The cloud cover had thickened since dusk, leaving the night moonless, and as McBride guided his horses away from the lake and toward a broad belt of pines on the east side of the lodge, Claire wondered how it was possible to see much of anything in the dark. Zachary had started out with his group shortly before and already had disappeared in the shadow of the trees, with only the bells on the horses' reins and the excited barking of the dogs to indicate the path he'd taken.

But when McBride emerged into open ground some five minutes later, she saw that the way ahead was illuminated with kerosene torches set at intervals on poles thrust into the snow.

"Kinda pretty, ain't it?" he said, stopping the sled briefly as they crested a little hill.

The countryside fell away before them, the faint sheen of the snow unbroken against the blackness of the sky except where the torches threw pools of yellow light on the narrow, winding road.

Pretty? The air was like champagne, the vastness of the landscape overwhelming. It was what she'd hoped to discover when she'd chosen to spend Christmas in Canada. In a word, it was magical. "Kinda," she breathed on a sigh, her attempt to imitate McBride leaving him rumbling with laughter.

Fifteen minutes later, they pulled up behind Zachary's sleigh. His passengers were gathered already under a tent-like structure whose heavy plastic sides were rolled up to allow people entry. Supported by cut lodgepole pine, it stood perhaps twelve meters high, with a vent in the center to allow the smoke to escape from the fire roaring in the pit below.

From her high perch next to McBride, Claire could see Melanie in the crowd, the tassels on her knitted cap bouncing merrily as she led Ian and Sue Dawson to a table where staff members were dispensing hot drinks and roasted chestnuts.

"This is it, folks, the end of the line. Everybody out." McBride pulled up the collar of his jacket, hauled a bulky object from behind the seat, and prepared to dismount. "If you'll hang on a minute, mamselle, I'll give you a hand climbing down."

Before he could act on the offer, Zachary materialized out of the shadows. "No need," he said. "I'll help her."

He stood beside the sleigh, a dark, unsmiling figure except where the fire threw swarthy highlights over his face. Deciding she'd rather deal with the devil, she ignored his outstretched hands and, stepping out onto the narrow running board, prepared to jump to the ground unaided. "*Merci*, but I really don't require your help, Zachary," she said haughtily.

"That's what you think," he said, and the next moment he had caught her by the waist and was swinging her through the air with such vigor that the breath came whooshing out of her lungs.

"I was perfectly capable of managing by myself," she huffed, staggering a little as he set her on her feet with rather more energy than was called for.

"And equally capable of breaking an ankle doing it, which is exactly the sort of thing we try to avoid having happen to our guests," he retorted, and fixed her in a penetrating stare. "I suppose I have you to thank for my daughter's latest attempt to look glamorous?"

Some perverse demon popped a reply into her mouth before she could contain it. "*Mon dieu*, don't tell me I've offended you yet again! What did it this time, Zachary? Is the sweater I lent her too red a reminder of a house of ill repute? Are you afraid its color might rob her of all moral rectitude?"

He looked down at his gloved hands and flexed them a little before saying in a low voice, "I guess I asked for that, but no, it wasn't what I had in mind at all. I was actually going to thank you. She looks good tonight, and a hell of a lot more presentable than if she'd been wearing that old sweater of mine that she's so taken with."

He had no right undermining her anger so easily. A mere apology should not be enough to erase his many slights, and only an idiot would let herself soften toward him. And yet, as she had almost from the moment they'd met, Claire found herself wishing that they could put aside their differences and admit to the attraction pulsing between them.

Perhaps he did, too, because he fumbled for her hand and said, "Claire, I make it a rule never to get involved with female guests, especially not with someone like you."

Someone like her? She bristled, any hint that they might

try to make a fresh start fading as fast as it had arisen. What did he mean, *someone like her?* By what standards had he decided she wasn't good enough to merit his attention when, his lofty protestations to the contrary, he flirted easily with every other woman present, including those old enough to be his mother?

I'd like to teach you a lesson, Zachary Alexander, she thought bitterly, *and just once leave you aching for me, as you left me yearning for you, last night.*

But vengeance was ugly and usually ended up generating more misery all round, so she straightened her spine and said coolly, "I'm glad you're pleased with how Melanie looks. Now, if you'll excuse me, I'd like to join the others."

She walked away quickly, aware that, for the first time in her life, she was really running away from herself.

She had been fourteen when she'd determined the standards by which she'd shape her future. Her mother had died in March, from causes not mentioned in decent society. The day after the funeral, Claire had returned to the seedy room behind the fish shop which had been home for as long as she could remember, and looked at the pitiful relics of Lisette's life: the tasteless, revealing blouses and short, too-tight skirts; the platform-soled shoes with their worn-down heels, the bright red lipstick and cheap perfume and outlandish orange rouge. All the trappings with which her poor mother had tried so desperately to buy love.

Claire had held them in her hands and cradled them to her in a way that her mother had never cradled her. And she had wept for a life that had ended where it had begun, less than thirty years earlier. In the gutter.

She had determined then that she would not fall victim to the same fate. Somehow, she would rise above her sordid beginnings. She would shake off the smells and the squalor which permeated the very pores of her skin and she would become *somebody*. Through her own efforts. With her self-respect intact. And she would succeed so completely that no one would ever think to question where she'd come from.

But of all the rules she'd laid down for herself that day, the most sacred had been that the only man who ever would know her body would be the man to whom she gave her heart—all of it, unconditionally, for as long as she lived. Yet the truth was, since she'd met Zachary Alexander, she'd been tempted to violate that edict, and the knowledge shook her.

A voice at her shoulder broke her reverie. "They've got hot chocolate on offer as well, but you're looking a bit down in the mouth and I thought this might restore your spirits."

"Oh," she said, finding Eric standing there, a stemmed cup of hot mulled wine in his hand, "it's you."

"Right. And before you tell me to get lost, please hear me out. My behavior last night was inexcusable and I'm sorry that you and Mel bore the brunt of it. It's a bit much to expect you to believe me when I say I won't overstep the mark again, so if you'd rather I kept my distance from here on, I'll understand. But I want you to know that if you need a friendly shoulder to lean on while you're here, you can count on me, no strings attached."

She had not imagined she would be glad to see him again, let alone welcome a reconciliation, but his obvious remorse touched her. From the moment she arrived, she'd been trying with singular lack of success to make amends to Zachary and knew well enough the frustration of having a sincere apology flung back in her face. She wouldn't resort to the same tactics now. "In that case," she said, drumming up a smile, "consider last night forgotten."

"Thanks." He nodded to where McBride, guitar slung over his lap, had taken his place near the fire while two other staff members passed around printed sheets of paper. "Would you like to sit down? It looks as if the entertainment's about to begin."

For the next while, as McBride led the crowd in one boisterous Christmas favorite after another, Claire was almost able to put aside her earlier despondency. But that changed the instant he segued into "Winter Wonderland."

The words of the song—of a man and a woman, in love and together in a place of unparalleled beauty at what was surely the most magical time of the year—stabbed her with a sudden, acute sadness. So many other Christmases she had survived being alone...how had it happened that this one was turning out so differently? Why did she feel as if she'd come close to finding something ineffably precious, only to lose it again?

Blinking furiously, she turned her head aside, loath to have anyone witness her distress. But someone did. Leaning against one of the lodgepole pine supports near the tent entrance, Zachary was watching her intently.

Trapped in his brooding, magnetic gaze, Claire floundered. Her throat dried up and the noise surrounding her fell into a strange silence broken only by the heavy, uneven thud of her heart. The misery inside faded away, consumed by an alien flame rivaling anything the kerosene torches could offer.

Desperately, she tried to swallow away the ache in her throat and could not. Just as desperately, she tried to tear her gaze loose. And could not. Instead, it roamed the features of his face, searching the inscrutable blue of his eyes, detailing the chiseled angle of his jaw, loving the sexy sweep of his mouth....

Loving? An involuntary gasp escaped her, a dry, hacking, painful inhalation of panic. There was that word again, sneaking up on her when she wasn't expecting it.

"What's up, Claire?" Eric inquired, touching her arm gently. "You choking on your hot wine, or something?"

Numbly, she shook her head. Across the tent, Zachary's glance flicked from Eric to the solicitous hand on her wrist, and his mouth tightened forbiddingly. Shoving himself away from the lodgepole pine support, he turned on his heel and ducked out of the tent, taking with him any semblance of warmth or connection the moment might have held.

McBride's was the lead sleigh on the journey back to the lodge, arriving some time before Zachary's. Pleading fatigue yet again, Claire refused Eric's invitation to join him for the midnight buffet. She wanted to be alone. Or more accurately, she did not want to be with him. But what she did want didn't bear thinking about.

Sleigh bells jingled faintly on the air and a moment later the two Samoyeds bounded out of the dark and raced toward the lodge. Like the coward she undoubtedly was, she hurried away before the other group came into sight because she couldn't face Zachary again until she'd regained control of her runaway emotions and, in her present state, it didn't seem likely to be something that would happen that night.

But escaping his physical presence didn't mean she could shut him out of her thoughts. No matter how fast she scurried away to her suite, or how deeply she snuggled under the down duvet, remembered moments with him—of words and looks and unspoken messages—followed her. How could she have laid up such a store of memories in so short a time?

You are a moth drawn to my flame, she'd said, the night she had arrived.

And you, he'd replied, the very air between them sizzling with awareness, *I suppose you're drawn to my flame, too?*

What if she'd said, *Yes. We don't know each other and yet I recognize in you something I've never found in any other man, something which speaks to my soul. Don't ask me to explain this because I cannot, any more than one side of a coin knows what lies on the other. And yet, they're joined together for all time. Perhaps we're the same: strangers destined to belong together.*

Would he have trained that intent gaze of his on her, and scoffed? Or would her courage have persuaded him to abandon his habitual reserve and look honestly into his own heart?

Just yesterday, when he'd asked for help with Melanie, she'd thought he'd come close to doing that. "Make her look special," he'd said, but it was what he hadn't said that had touched her. *Like you,* his gaze had implied.

Had she read too much into the exchange? Did a woman lose all perspective when the right man, the *only* man, came into her life? And was he that man? How could she be sure?

So the unsettling thoughts circled through her mind, broken only by the sound of Melanie coming home shortly before one o'clock and calling softly to the dogs. A long time later, a man's heavier footsteps sounded on the back veranda and a door closed with a quiet thud. And still Claire lay in her bed, as wide awake as if it had been noon and the sun shining full on her face, with her foolish heart racing because only a wall separated her from him.

Did he sleep naked? When he made love to a woman, did he hold her captive with his strong thighs? Did his hands explore her while his mouth tasted her? How many women had known the feel of him buried inside them? Would she become one of that number?

Shocked beyond measure by such wild imaginings, Claire popped up in the bed like a cork tossed by an incoming ocean wave. Throwing aside the duvet, she searched out her swimsuit. Ungoverned thoughts of Zachary Alexander would never cure her insomnia but, fortunately, a more effective and infinitely less disturbing remedy lay close at hand.

Clutching a towel and wearing a thick terry-cloth robe and her boots, she eased open the sliding glass door overlooking the lake. Ignoring the cold biting clean through to her bones, she made her way along a narrow path cleared of snow to the deck where the whirlpool stood.

To one side of it was a small open shelter, scarcely high enough for a grown man to stand upright. But inside was a bench with a row of hooks on the wall above it, both clearly intended to protect footwear, robes and towels from the weather. Even better, the structure screened a bather from the windows at Zachary's end of the building.

Not that she expected him to be looking out. Beyond the faint icy glow of the lake, there wasn't a flicker of light showing anywhere. Even the miniature mushroom-shaped flood lamps surrounding the spa deck had been turned off for the night.

Removing her robe and boots, she lifted back the hinged lid of the tub then, before she froze to death, quickly lowered herself up to her chin in the hot, steamy depths and turned on the jets. She could think of little she'd like less than being found by Zachary the next morning, blue with cold and stiff as a board.

The water swirled and rumbled around her, massaging the small of her back, her shoulders, the tense, angry muscles in her neck. Letting out a long, relaxing breath, she rested her head on the edge of the tub and gazed at the sky. The clouds had shredded, exposing great bursts of stars, yet the air was filled with ice crystals so fine they resembled sparkling motes of silver.

It was the glitter dust that undid her, dazzling her with its perfect brilliance so that her vision became blinded with rainbows, and leaving her heart aching. So much of her life had been filled with an ugliness she'd never wanted to share with a man. But this! Such pure and pristine beauty was designed for lovers to enjoy together. And she was alone....

"How come you're lying there with your eyes shut? Don't you know you're missing one of the greatest shows on earth?" His voice, as deep and dark as the shadows which had concealed his approach, was close enough that she heard it clearly over the sound of the water jets. Close enough that it feathered her ear as warmly as the water massaged her body.

Somehow, she contained her yelp of surprise. And somehow, by the time she'd turned her head and was face-to-face with him as he sat on his heels at the edge of the pool, she'd managed to wipe most of the misery from her expression. What was wrong with her, anyhow? She'd never been a weeper, having learned long ago that tears did nothing but undermine a person's resolve. Why this recent tendency to dissolve without warning over minor tragedies?

In place of the navy snowmobile suit he'd had on earlier, he wore a pair of soft denim jeans, a heavy turtleneck sweater and leather après-ski boots. As if he didn't already look more beautiful than any man had a right to, a few ice crystals clung to him, just enough to highlight his thick, dark hair and draw attention to the width of his shoulders.

She swallowed and murmured, "Hello," because it was all she could think of to say.

"Hi," he said. Just that, his breath wreathing around her

head in little frozen puffs, and she wondered how it was possible that he could render such a little, inconsequential word into something so full of vibrant intent.

A silence followed, filled with unspoken things; things that had to do with a man and a woman, which they'd never let themselves say and which, suddenly, didn't matter anymore because a deeper, more intimate understanding surged between them.

Beside him on the rim of the tub he had placed another towel and a pair of high-soled sabots made of some kind of plastic. He took the towel and rolled it into a cylinder. Then he turned her so that she was faced away from him again, and pulled her head back until it rested against the towel at the nape of her neck. "Look up," he said.

She did, and this time could not contain her gasp. The sky was shot through with streams of light, the kind she'd seen on the little holy pictures given to her by the nuns at the convent where, for one brief time, she'd gone to school when she was seven. Rose pink and clear aquamarine and frosty, swirling white, they rode the night with their beams. "What is it?" she whispered, awestruck.

"The northern lights," he said, and she realized that he had cupped her jaw and was stroking his fingers lightly up and down the length of her throat. "We see them often up here, but I don't think any of us ever lose our sense of wonder at them."

Still gazing at the sky, she said, "Do you believe in miracles, Zachary?"

"I don't know. Do you?"

"Yes," she said. "I would think that anyone seeing this would have no choice *but* to believe in them. Why did you come down here?"

"I couldn't sleep and when I heard the jets come on, I knew you couldn't, either. And I thought...."

"Oui?"

The pressure of his fingers increased fractionally, as though he were struggling to clear a last hurdle of reservation about her. She waited, her heart trembling with hope and the rest of her melting in the tactile pleasure of his touch.

And then he withdrew his hands and she could have wept with disappointment. "I brought a pair of clogs for you to wear back to the house," he said. "I wasn't sure you'd found those in the guest suite or that you'd know what they were for."

She heard him move away and for one dreadful second thought he was leaving her as suddenly as he'd arrived. Then he came back and touched her hair. "Come out now, Claire. You've been in there long enough."

She looked over her shoulder and saw him holding open her robe. Saw the towel slung over his arm, and the sabots waiting to receive her bare, wet feet. But most of all, she saw the look on his face and knew that he had not even begun to tell her all that was on his mind.

Rising from the steam, she reached out to him. He took her hand and pulled her up beside him and wrapped her in the robe. And without either of them saying another word, he took her to the guest suite and opened the door, and when they were both inside, he closed it again and turned the lock.

CHAPTER EIGHT

DIMLY, it occurred to Zach, in that part of his brain still functioning with a modicum of reason, that he should say something. Explain why: why he'd come looking for her, why he'd given in to the attraction he'd been so determined to resist, and most of all, why now, when their alienation had never been more complete.

He could have made excuses; said that the reason he'd come down to the spa deck was to show her how to override the timer for the mini-floodlights so that she could operate them manually and not have to stumble around in the dark. But no amount of subterfuge explained the desire which, wisdom and reason be damned, arced between him and her. The simple truth was, they'd wanted each other from the first and pretending otherwise had done nothing but leave the hunger so rapacious that it had finally taken them hostage.

So he said nothing. Instead, he looked at her. Looked his fill, openly for a change instead of covertly, and not giving a damn that she, in turn, was looking at him and could see the passion he no longer cared to disguise.

A lamp burning in the living room threw a faint glow into the hall, just enough to delineate the sweep of her lower lip, the curve of one eyebrow, the shadow of her lashes on her cheek. In the half-light he skimmed his finger down one side of the vee opening of her robe and up the other.

At that, a shudder rippled over her and she let her head fall back, offering the smooth, vulnerable length of her throat to his touch. He leaned forward and pressed his mouth in the hollow where her collarbones met, at the spot just below her chin, at the corner of her jaw.

She let out a sound—not quite a sigh, not quite a moan, but unmistakably compliant—and swayed toward him. Sliding his hands down her arms, he found the knot of the tie belt at her waist and loosened it, and the next moment she was where he'd wanted her for longer than he'd been willing to admit, in his arms, with her damp, exquisite body pressed against his and him so hard he thought he'd explode.

Uncaring that her skin smelled of chlorine or that the dripping ends of her hair plastered themselves to his cheek, he explored her mouth, tasting its secrets and marveling at its sweetness. And wondering if he could hold himself in check long enough to carry her down the hall to the bedroom or if he was going to make love to her there, on the floor.

The slight pebble of goose bumps beneath his hands made the decision for him, shaming him into realizing that she was clammy with cold beneath her wetly clinging swimsuit. Picking her up, he strode down the hall and into the bathroom.

Reaching inside the glass-enclosed shower stall, he turned on the water and adjusted the temperature. Happening to glance in the mirror, he saw that she stood where he'd left her, her eyes unnaturally bright, her face too pale except for two spots of color high on her cheeks, and her hands plucking distractedly at the lapels of her robe. If he hadn't known the absurdity of such an idea, he'd have thought she was nervous.

"Strip off those wet things," he said. "Even if you weren't chilled to the bone, you need to rinse off the chlorine from the spa. It's not good for your skin."

She nodded and swung her gaze from him to the door. In case that didn't say plainly enough that she wanted to be alone, she hugged the robe modestly close to her body. Taking the hint, he said, "While you're doing that, I'll fix us a drink."

She had nothing in the bar except for what the resort supplied and he ought to check on Mel anyway so, making sure he left the guest suite door off the latch, he let himself into his own place. Lily rose up from her habitual spot outside Mel's door but Blanche, the more territorial of the two dogs, remained stretched out in front of the family room fireplace and acknowledged him only with a single thump of her tail, sign enough that all was well under his roof.

He found a bottle of cognac he'd been saving for a special occasion, stopped by Mel's room long enough to pull the duvet up over her shoulders, and was back in Claire's suite within ten minutes, half expecting and half hoping she'd still be in the shower.

But instead of the muted sluice of water hitting the glass enclosure, the whine of a hair dryer filtered toward him and he found her in front of the mirror in her bedroom. She had put on something long and flowing, with wide sleeves. A caftan, he thought it was called, made out of silk probably, and patterned with swirls of dark purple and a deep forest green against which her skin glowed like a pearl.

To his relief, a couple of fat candles glimmered on the dresser and one more on the bedside table. A woman who'd changed her mind about making love with a man didn't light candles. Still, he stood there in the doorway like a kid about to embark on his first sexual experience and not certain of the protocol involved.

She met his glance in the mirror and smiled, a soft and tentative lift of her lips that left him hollow with hunger.

Then, unplugging the dryer and laying down her hairbrush, she bent to blow out the two candles on the dresser.

He didn't like to think he was a man so bent on self-gratification that he didn't care about ensuring a woman's pleasure, but the erotic grace with which she went about her task—the way she cupped her hand around each flame and pursed her mouth to puff out a breath, the supple bow of her spine, the shadowed cleft between her breasts revealed as she leaned forward—infected him with a kind of madness.

Suddenly, everything had gone on too long: the feuding, the sparring, the resisting. And most of all, the denying.

In two strides, he was at her side. Filling his hands with the silky stuff of her gown, lifting it over her head, shedding his own clothes with unparalleled speed, lowering her to the mattress—those preliminary rituals ordinarily demanding a certain finesse, passed in a blur. They didn't matter. He was too consumed with his own need.

God help him, he paid no attention to anything but the slender weight of her breasts in his palm; the scent of her skin—flowers now, where before there'd been chlorine; the warm flavor of her made all the sweeter by the involuntary spasm that took hold of her when he tasted her; his own pulsing response when she touched him, holding him lightly and driving him mad with her delicate, exploring fingers.

"Ah, Claire," he groaned, "you're killing me!" And spreading her legs wide so that he could nest between them, he went to bury himself inside her, nearly shattering at the snug embrace with which she received him.

Not once did he stop to wonder, to ask. Not until he met the faint but unmistakable resistance to his entering her did it occur to him to do either, and by then it was too late.

Any movement, even the act of trying to withdraw, provoked too much ecstasy. Or agony. Or both.

And the way she clung to him, and lifted herself to meet him, and drew him into her regardless of her own discomfort and whether or not he had any right to be there, and hooked her legs over his hips until she was all around him, tight and silken and hot—what chance did he stand of reversing matters then, when the damage was already done?

None, that's what. He was at the mercy of the passion which took hold, of the frantic rhythm driving him too hard, too briefly, too soon. While she lay beneath him, hanging on for dear life because she didn't know what else to expect, he exploded inside her, out of control and out of bounds. No condom, no nothing, except post-climactic shudders racking his body and guilt chewing holes in his mind.

Burying his face in her hair, he tried to drown out the voices coming at him from every direction, pointing the finger of blame. Shaming him. But there was no forgiving the unforgivable. He had taken a virgin. Again.

In one swift leap, time sped backward to another Christmas, one that had ended up changing the entire course of his life....

Jenny had been nineteen when they met, and paying for her season's pass by working in the cafeteria at the coastal resort where he'd been a ski pro. He'd noticed her the first day, asked her out the next, and given her free lessons on her afternoons off because she barely knew how to snowplow, let alone tackle a mogul. And lured her to bed the following week, never dreaming he'd be her first lover because it was a well established fact that the ski bunnies littering the beginners' hill were there as much for the action off the slopes as on.

By the time he graduated with his MBA the following May, she was five months pregnant. With nothing but his degree and her absolute faith in his ability to make her happy, they'd married and she'd put full-time motherhood ahead of her plans to become a teacher. "There'll be time for that later, when the baby's in school," she'd said.

Later had come when Mel turned eight and they could practically taste Easy Street. It had ended then, too, with Jenny dead on a crosswalk in Vancouver and the husband and child she'd adored not there to tell her one last time that they loved her.

But not once in all those years had he known the drowning passion that consumed him now. "I'm so sorry, Jenny!" he mumbled, regret and guilt overwhelming him to the point that he'd spoken the words aloud before he realized it.

In the seconds that followed, it seemed to him that everything stopped. Reality, time, his heartbeat, all got swallowed up in a black, immobilizing pause during which he prayed that his voice had been too muffled for what he'd said to make any sense to Claire lying soft and pliant as honey beneath him.

She heard perfectly though, and before his words had cooled on the air, she changed from clinging warmth to aloof withdrawal.

"Claire!" he said, trying to hold onto her. "I didn't mean that the way it sounded."

But it was like trying to hold a shadow. She slid from under him and rushed out of the room, snatching up the duvet on the way. Hauling on his undershorts, he raced after her, cursing.

He found her on the hearth in the living room, the way she huddled beneath the quilt clutched haphazardly around her shoulders, with her hair hanging down her back in wild

curls and her eyes gazing sightlessly at the flames, reminding him of a painting he'd once seen of a street urchin
crouching for warmth next to a brazier in some dark alley.

Hunkering down next to her, he touched her arm.
"Claire? Sweetheart?"

She flinched as if he'd struck her.

Closing his eyes, he struggled to find words that would
make things right again. "Look," he said finally, "I wish
I could undo what just happened, but I can't. All I can tell
you is that it had nothing to do with you. With us."

"Us?" She turned her head in slow motion and fixed
him in an empty, bottomless stare. "There is no us. There
never was."

"You're wrong," he said. "For a little while, there was
only us. No one else."

"I'm not interested in a little while," she said bleakly.
"And I'm not interested in being your surrogate lover. If
all I want is to be used, I can think of a dozen men who'd
be pleased to have me service them without their feeling
the need to remind me that I am, at best, a substitute for
the woman they'd prefer to be with."

She leveled him with her pain. *Service?* he wanted to
roar. *We made love, damn it!*

But he kept quiet because there were no words to make
things right. There never would be. With a slip of the
tongue that was both more complex and more complimentary than she could begin to guess, he had destroyed any
chance they might have had for a relationship that lasted
beyond the next few days.

In the long run, it was probably best this way, he acknowledged gloomily. Because, now that he'd managed to
drag his brain above his waist and back where it belonged,
how the hell did he think polar opposites such as they were

could find a common meeting ground on which to base anything but the most fleetingly casual encounter?

They couldn't, and they'd be fools to try. European sophisticate and Canadian workingman made for a bad mix, no matter how positive a spin you tried to put on it. But that hardly exonerated him from the fallout of what had just occurred between them. "It was your first time," he said, feeling obligated to broach the one subject he'd most have liked to avoid.

"Don't be silly," she said. "Of course it wasn't."

"Yes, it was, Claire. You were a virgin."

She yawned delicately, like a small pedigreed cat bored to tears by the bumbling attention of the randy tom from next door. "Once, perhaps, a long time ago."

Stymied, he glared at her, inclined to remind her of the modesty she'd exhibited in the bathroom and which, too much after the fact, had given the first hint of her innocence. But what good would it serve, if she was determined to deny the truth?

He paced to the window and back again. "Okay, we'll let that pass for now. But what happens next?"

"I intend taking a very long, cleansing bath," she said. "As for you, you can boil in oil, for all I care."

"Will you cut your stay here short?"

She raised her chin disdainfully. "Certainly not. Why should I?"

"Because it's damn near impossible to avoid running into each other in a place this size and, feeling as you do, you'd probably prefer not to have to see me again."

"You did a splendid job of avoiding me before tonight, Zachary, and I see no reason for you not to continue to do so. The pity of it is that you allowed lust to supersede your disaffection for me, but I'm confident you won't make the same mistake again. And if you're worried that I might make a nuisance of myself, I can assure you that your fears are groundless. I'd rather sleep with a...a...boa constrictor than repeat tonight's mistake with you.''

The words fell out of her mouth like pebbles hitting glass: distinct, precise, and stilted as hell. If it hadn't been for the occasional hesitation as she struggled to translate her thoughts into the sort of faultless high-flown English a duchess might resort to, he'd have thought she'd rehearsed the speech at least a dozen times.

''And what if you're pregnant?'' he said, the awful possibility arising to confront him like the ghost it was.

''I almost certainly am not. But even if I were, so what?''

Stunned as much by her attitude as the question itself, he stared at her. ''*So what?* We're talking about a life here, Claire, one that would be as much my responsibility as yours.''

''No,'' she said. ''Your responsibility was not to have sex with me and pretend I was someone else. In choosing to ignore that, you forfeited any rights you might otherwise have had.''

Practically choking on frustration, he said, ''This happens to be Canada, my dear, and the law disagrees with you. Fathers have the same rights as mothers in this country.''

In one lithe movement she was on her feet, the duvet draped around her like a toga, her posture so erect she might have had a yardstick taped to her spine. ''Do they?'' she said, and snapped her fingers under his nose. ''Well, that is what I think of Canada and its laws. They and you can go to hell, Zachary!''

Go to 'ell, Zacharree!

I'm already there, he felt like telling her. And whether you're willing to admit it or not, so are you!

But he'd caused enough upheaval for one night, so all he said was, "We'll see about that."

"Go away," she said.

"I will. For now. But I'll be back."

"Don't bother," she said. "You have nothing to say that I wish to hear."

"Forget it, Claire. We'll talk this whole thing out tomorrow. Maybe by then you'll be more inclined to listen to reason."

At the very least, he'd hoped to make a dignified exit but she snookered him on that, too. Marching into the bedroom, she returned within seconds, his jeans, socks, sweater and boots heaped in the crook of one arm. "Clearly, you have difficulty understanding my English, so perhaps this will make my meaning clearer."

And opening the front door, she hurled his clothing out on the deck without once losing her grip on the duvet clutched modestly to her breasts. His boots followed in short order, landing with a muffled thump at the top of the steps.

"For crying out loud, Claire!" He blinked, not quite believing his eyes, then turned to confront her. "Have you lost your mind?"

By way of reply, she fired off a stream of rapid French and picked up her next missile which happened to be a heavy brass candlestick. It didn't take a rocket scientist to figure out that what she'd said could in no way be construed as complimentary.

Deciding that discretion was definitely the better part of valor, he backed out of range. The minute his bare feet touched the frost-glazed wooden boards of the deck, she slammed the door in his face and locked it.

He scooped up his things and was about to make a beeline for his own front door when he noticed the steam rising

from the spa. In his haste to get her into bed, he'd forgotten
to replace the cover on the tub. More important, he hadn't
checked to make sure the insulated door covering the
Jacuzzi control panel had been closed. If it hadn't and the
pipes froze, he'd be facing major repair bills by the morning.

Swearing, he struggled into his jeans, shoved his feet into
his boots, and yanked his sweater over his head before the
minus forty degree temperature rendered him chronically
impotent. That done, he hustled his sorry rear down to the
spa deck, closed up the hot tub and made sure the equipment was weatherproof.

Apart from the hum of the water heater, the night was
quiet; calm and bright, as the carol said. The cloud had
completely disappeared, leaving the sky thick with stars and
the air so sharp and clear, it almost rang.

This was what his life was really all about, he reminded
himself, stopping for one last look around: the permanent
tangibles of guest houses tucked into the fold of the lakeshore to his left, the great chimneys of the main lodge lifting clear of the pines behind him, and his daughter sleeping
safe in her bed not twenty feet away.

And Claire Durocher? He raked his fingers through his
hair and heaved a sigh. She was merely passing through, a
temporary aberration neither anxious nor able to impact his
ordered existence. So why couldn't he dismiss her and
chalk the evening up to a combination of bad luck and bad
judgment?

From somewhere beyond the far reaches of the lake came
the prolonged, soul-stirring howl of a wolf. It was a sound
whose wild loneliness always moved him, but never as it
did that night, with the tactile memory of her still imprinted
on his body.

Dismiss her? He had about as much chance of doing that

as he had of walking into his house to discover Santa Claus climbing down the chimney!

She woke the next morning to narrow shafts of sunlight spearing through the slits in the bedroom blinds and the sound of voices echoing from the lake. Propping herself up on one elbow, she squinted at the clock and saw that it was almost eleven.

How, she wondered groggily, could she have slept half the day away? And why did she ache as if she'd skied the Matterhorn the day before?

The memories came tumbling over her then—of his big, warm hands gentle on her body, his voice, smoky with desire, luring her to break the vow she'd kept all these years. And of her not caring because, in the small hours of the morning when she'd found herself so unaccountably bereft, he'd come to her and made sense of the loneliness.

If only she'd had the wit or strength to call a halt to things and very firmly close the door to her suite while he was still on the other side! But she had not, and like a film unwinding, later images crowded in, of clothing cast haphazardly over the carpet, and limbs spread indecently on the bed; of pulsing rhythm and a throat burned dry by passion; of a voice, *her* voice, uttering deep guttural pleas, and her hands bent on outrageous discovery.

Her body quivered, clutched by an involuntary spasm as she recalled how she'd let him touch her, intimately, with his mouth, until some invisible spring inside her had coiled tighter and tighter on itself and finally burst free of its own restraints, leaving her too dazed to care whether she lived or died as long as she could feel his warmth covering her and filling her.

How naive she'd been to think that he'd wanted her as she'd wanted him! How ill-advised to have welcomed the brief, sharp discomfort as he entered her in the belief that the pleasure which followed was worth any amount of pain. And how quickly she'd paid the price for such foolishness.

Jenny, he'd called her, crying out the name when he was buried so deep inside her that he'd seemed to touch her soul.

Jenny!

Once, when she was about eleven, she'd overheard her mother talking to another woman, a friend who often waited with her at the end of the alley, on long, hot summer evenings when dusk lay thick on Marseilles.

"I never ask their names," Lisette had said. "It's easier just to call them all 'lover'. That way you don't get one mixed up with another."

Claire hadn't really understood what her mother had meant at the time, but she understood now. And oh, *mon dieu*, how the knowledge hurt!

She might have fallen back into bed then and wept for the misery of it all, had there not come a knock at the front door. But whatever else she'd squandered, her pride remained intact. She would neither hide herself away nor betray her distress to anyone else by so much as the flicker of an eyelid.

Hastily pulling on her robe, she stopped at the dresser just long enough to draw a brush through her hair. Not that it improved her appearance any. She didn't need the mirror to tell her she looked like hell, but that, she supposed, was the price one paid for throwing a lifetime of caution to the winds for a few brief moments of ecstasy.

One of the women from the beauty spa waited outside on the veranda. "Sorry to disturb you, Miss Durocher," she said. "I'm Liz and I gave you your facial yesterday."

"I remember," Claire said. "What can I do for you now?"

"Zach noticed you missed breakfast this morning and asked me to come by to make sure you're okay. He'd have come himself, but he's too busy, it being Christmas Eve and all."

Too busy to show a little sensitivity? Too indifferent to how she might be feeling, now that he'd got what he wanted out of her? Or too busy chasing after new quarry?

Those and a dozen other pithy retorts sprang to Claire's mind but she recognized the injustice of heaping them on this woman's hapless head.

"You may tell him," she said, "that I am perfectly well, thank you, and that his concern is misdirected—especially in view of the many other more important matters occupying his mind on this particular day."

"But you do look a little pale, Miss Durocher. If you're feeling the least bit off-color, we have a doctor on call and I'd be glad to make an appointment for him to see you."

To do what? Confirm what she already knew: that she'd thrown away her virginity on someone who'd forgotten who it was lying beneath him, almost before he'd had his way with her? Because Zachary had been right, damn him! He had been the first man with whom she'd made love.

Made love? She drew in a pained breath. They had not made love, they'd had sex and if anyone ought to know the difference, it was she, given her upbringing.

"I don't need a doctor, Liz," she said, squaring her shoulders. "I partied late last night and slept the morning away to make up for it, that's all. When you see Mr. Alexander, please let him know that—"

"Actually, I won't be seeing him, at least not for some time. He left the resort about an hour ago and isn't expected back until later this afternoon."

Well, that was an unexpected blessing! She hadn't eaten

in nearly fifteen hours and was starving, but bumping into him at lunch would have been enough to kill her appetite.

And tonight, when everyone gathered for the Christmas Eve festivities and there was no avoiding him, what then? Why, she'd do what she did best: put on a front to hide the pain inside. She'd wear the violet silk moire shot through with blue and green, and the antique faux emerald jewelry studded with Austrian crystals. She'd laugh and dance and be so full of Christmas good cheer that no one would guess she was hiding a broken heart.

As for Zachary Alexander, he could go hang himself! The moon would turn to cheese before she'd spare him another glance. Because she'd rather be dead than give him the idea that she was languishing for his attentions. His most enduring impressions of her would be of a woman too busy having fun with other people to care one iota about his whereabouts or doings.

At lunch, she met a Melanie firmly under the spell of first love, and if the smitten look in Ian Dawson's eye was any indication, the feeling was mutual.

Straight-faced, Claire said, "Why don't you and I go cross-country skiing this afternoon, Melanie?"

"Gee, Claire, it's not that I wouldn't like to, but I sort of planned to go skating with Ian. But you could come with us, if you like."

She looked so crestfallen that Claire felt guilty for teasing her. "I was joking, *chérie*! I'm sure your beau would be most disappointed if you brought along a chaperone."

"Oh." Obviously relieved, Melanie confided, "He wanted to know what my favorite color is and I saw him looking around the gift shop earlier. I think he might be going to get me a Christmas gift. And he asked if I'd sit with him at dinner tonight."

"You said yes, of course?"

The pink cheeks turned even rosier. "Yes. It's my first ever date, Claire, and—"

"And once again, you don't have a thing to wear!" It felt good to laugh, to realize that life didn't start and end with this sweet child's father. "Then we must put our heads together and see what we can find."

"You'd do that for me again?"

"Yes, if you'll do me a favor and tell me which are the best cross-country trails to follow this afternoon."

"I'll do better than that," Melanie said. "I'll draw you a map. My favorite is one that none of the visitors ever bothers with because it looks pretty steep at the start and it takes the whole afternoon to complete the loop. But it's worth the climb and there's a warming hut at the top with the best view in the world. It's where I go when I want to get away from everybody. It's really peaceful and there's always chocolate and snacks and stuff in the supply bin because no one ever uses the place. It's a neat place to rest before you follow the trail back down to the valley."

She hadn't exaggerated, Claire thought, a couple of hours later. The view from the little deck outside the warming hut was worth every arduous minute it had taken to get there. The trees were frozen confections, the sky a huge cobalt bowl upturned over mountain peaks so jagged and endless that one had to wonder how any man had found the courage to explore so vast a landscape.

What was it Zachary had said in answer to her complaints, the day she arrived? That Switzerland would fit more than twenty times into British Columbia alone? Well, from this perspective, she could well believe it. Such enduring serenity was balm to her soul and if it weren't that she'd promised to meet Melanie at the guest suite by five o'clock, she'd have been happy to stay and soak in the ambience until dusk fell, and then to curl up on one of the two cots in the warming hut, with nothing but the wood stove and one of the sleeping bags stored there for emergencies, to keep her company for the night.

But, a promise was a promise, especially to a child, and not something to be broken because a man had turned one's life upside down. Reluctantly, she strapped on her skis and with one last look at the splendor around her, set off along the winding trail which the map showed would bring her out just a kilometer or two north of the resort.

The return trip was much less strenuous and she reached the valley as the sun was lowering over the lake. It hung just above the horizon, a ball of fire staining the ice with flaming color and flinging the tall outline of the lodge into dark relief.

Had it not made such a magnificent sight, she might have paid more attention to the path in front of her and noticed Zachary coming toward her. She might not have been so dazzled by the brilliance of light that she couldn't determine the expression on his face. But she would have had to be both deaf and stupid not to hear the controlled anger in his voice as he accosted her.

"Is this your idea of teaching me a lesson, Claire?" he snarled. Yes, he snarled. Like a wild dog about to attack. And in light of their last encounter, she found his manner unpardonable.

"Don't growl at me like that," she said, sounding like a snappish little poodle herself, "because I won't stand for it."

"And I won't stand for the kind of reckless behavior you've engaged in this afternoon," he said, not moderating his tone in the slightest. "What the hell were you thinking of, taking off by yourself in terrain you're completely unfamiliar with? Well?'' He bore down on her, a tall, forbidding figure in the unrelieved black of his outfit. ''Are you really as brainless as you seem, or was this a calculated attempt to punish me for last night?''

CHAPTER NINE

CLAIRE planted her ski poles in the snow and with a commendable show of indifference said, "Believe it or not, Zachary, thoughts of you didn't so much as enter my mind. I wanted to explore the cross-country trails and I had a very pleasant afternoon doing so—until now."

Of course, she wasn't being entirely truthful. For all her attempts to shut him out, he'd crept into her thoughts much too often but she had no intention of admitting it. If she couldn't control her emotions, she could certainly keep a rein on her tongue.

"You should have told someone," he snapped. "As a guest at this resort, you have an obligation to keep us informed of where you are and when you expect to return."

"Don't use that tone with me," she shot back. "I'm an adult, not a child. And it just so happens that Melanie knew where I'd gone and when I planned to return."

"But Melanie *is* a child and you had no business saddling her with the responsibility for your welfare."

"You dare to speak to me of responsibility, Zachary? You, who sought me out last night and only after you'd had your way with me, thought to ask if you could possibly have made me pregnant?"

She hadn't thought him a man who would blush easily but, at her words, a splash of darker color stained the tanned skin stretched over his cheekbones. He started to speak, then changed his mind and drawing in a short, sharp breath, looked away from her to study the mountain peaks rearing up beyond the far reaches of the lake.

She could see the conflicting expressions chasing over his features—the guilt, the anger, the regret—but she was still too emotionally fragile herself to spare him much sympathy. Yet it wasn't in her nature to hold a grudge. For all that it had wounded her, she knew he hadn't intended to slight her with his inadvertent reference to his dead wife, and a part of her wanted to reach out to him now and forgive the lapse.

To do so, however, would be to invite more misery. She didn't know if it was possible to fall in love with a man she'd met only a few days earlier, but she knew with utter certainty that the feelings he aroused in her were unlike anything she'd ever experienced before.

She wanted to give to this man. She would, she realized shakily, have given him anything he asked of her, and if she possessed one scrap of self-preservation, she'd remove herself from the possibility of succumbing to such temptation. If she was to walk away from Topaz Valley reasonably heart-whole, she must see to it that she was never again alone with him.

Propelling herself forward on her skis, she went to move past him. But at the last moment, he barred her way. "We need to talk about last night," he said, holding her firmly by the wrist.

"There's more to say?" She tossed her head dismissively. "I think not. I think you said enough already."

"I'm not proud of how I behaved, Claire, but you've got to know that what I said had nothing to do with you."

"Of course I know that," she said scornfully. "It had to do with your wife. With Jenny."

"Only in a very small way. When I came down to the hot tub, it wasn't Jenny I was looking for, it was you. It was you I wanted when we went back to your suite, you I needed and held in my arms, and—"

"No!" she cried, her emotions stripped raw by the memories he was bent on reviving. "You're a man still married to the past, Zachary, which is why there's no point in our discussing the matter further, because I do not involve myself with married men."

"Jenny's been dead for nearly six years, for God's sake!"

"Not in your heart. You speak of what *you* want, what *you* need, but what about me?" She paused, debating the wisdom of continuing for fear of inviting further hurt. But what had started between them as sexual attraction had developed into a deeper issue, one that had to do with moral principles.

By going to bed with him, she had reneged on one of her most sacred promises to herself. She would not compromise her self-respect further by lying to him now. "You see me as selfish and spoiled—"

"I never said that."

"But you thought it. You decided the moment you met me that I was...how do you say it in English? A spoiled bat?"

"A brat," he said, and she thought he might be biting his lips to keep from smiling. "Okay, I admit it. I thought that."

"Well, you weren't entirely wrong. I decided a long time ago what I want for myself, and I'm not about to make do with half measures. I don't want a room when I've reserved a suite. And I don't want a man's body without his heart."

He looked nonplussed. "You surely didn't expect me to propose, just because we made...?"

"Love," she supplied, when he seemed about to gag on the word. "Except that we didn't—make love, that is. We made a hay roll."

"You mean a roll in the hay," he said, dazedly.

She shrugged. "No matter. The point is, if it had been love we were making, you wouldn't have called out to your dead wife, and I wouldn't have been left feeling...inexpensive."

"Cheap. You wouldn't feel cheap." As if he'd just woken and was trying to clear his mind of a bad dream, he shook his head. "How did a discussion about our...*involvement* turn into an English lesson?"

"I'm sure I don't know. Nor can I waste any more time helping you to find out because I have an appointment with Melanie."

"What for?"

"To help her prepare for tonight. She wants to look her best and I agreed to help her again."

"Well, she won't have to borrow your clothes this time," he said, seeming relieved to change the subject. "While I was in Broome this morning, I bought her a dress more suited to her age."

The admission was enough to give a woman pause. "What does that mean, Zachary? That you bought her a little girl's party dress, with pink frills and a matching ribbon for her hair?"

"Give me credit for having some sense! I've seen the way she looks at the Dawson boy. She's past the little-girl stage, more's the pity."

"What a comfort to know that you're not entirely lacking in perception!" Claire retorted, and with a deceptively airy wave, she skied away.

This time he made no effort to detain her.

Dinner was a stunning success. Beluga caviar and artichokes, stuffed quail, and grilled wild salmon served with asparagus all deserved rave reviews especially when, as a grand finale, Roberto and his sous-chefs appeared and, with all but the lights on the tree extinguished, wove a path among the tables, carrying silver trays of baked Alaska topped by flaming sparklers.

After the meal, the party moved to the lounge where a trio from town had been hired to supply live music for the next three nights. From his spot near the door, Zach cast a practiced eye over the room and saw that the same standard of excellence applied here as in the dining room.

Huge flower arrangements filled the Chinese vases set on jardinieres between the tall windows. The exotic scent of imported plumeria, roses and carnations mingled with the aromatic tang of mandarin oranges and wood smoke. Champagne flutes gleamed in the light of numerous candles placed randomly on the mantelpiece, the occasional tables, the piano and any other surface large enough to accommodate a holder.

Already, the small dance floor was crowded. He saw Melanie and the Dawson boy bobbing around energetically in some sort of ritual performance he assumed was meant to represent dancing. Mel's cheeks were flushed, her eyes bright. Her mouth had lost its sullen droop and for the first time in too long, she looked happy. A month ago, that would have been enough to make him content.

Clutching a beer stein in one hand, McBride ambled over from the bar to join him and gave him an elbow in the ribs. "Pretty as a picture, ain't she?"

She was, although he hadn't been sure he'd made the best choice until she'd shown up for dinner. But as soon as he saw her, he knew he'd got it right and she knew it, too. She'd walked up to him without once looking as if she might fall out of her borrowed sandals, and thrown her arms around his neck.

"Thanks, Daddy," she'd whispered, and he'd found himself embarrassingly choked up at being the father of this beautiful young stranger who smelled of flowers and looked so grown up with her hair pinned in place by some sort of jeweled brooch and her fingernails shaped into smooth pink ovals.

"Yeah," he said to McBride. "That dark red color really suits her."

"I'm not talking about Mel, boy, and well you know it." McBride settled his gaze on Claire and, unwillingly, Zach followed suit.

She sat with several other guests at a table next to the fireplace, the laughter spilling out and flooding her face with warmth. He wanted to catch her expression and freeze-frame it in his mind for when she'd gone back to that other, more glamorous world, and all he had left of her was the memory of this Christmas.

"Why don't you stop tormentin' yourself and go ask her to dance before somebody else beats you to it?" McBride suggested.

"Because she'd probably tell me to take a hike," he said, mesmerized by the way the flames made her dress seem to change from blue to green to purple as she moved her head and shoulders, and sent sparks of brilliant color shooting from the jewels swinging at her ears. "We're not on the best of terms."

"Do tell! And how much longer you aimin' to keep this up, Zach?"

He shifted from one foot to the other. "I don't know what you mean."

McBride let out a cackle. "Hell, I might not be the brightest light on the tree, but I can tell when a man and a woman fit together snug as two bugs in a rug, and sonny, I'm seein' two now, 'cept there's about thirty feet of floor space separatin' them."

"You're wrong," he said. "I can't give her what she's looking for."

There was a moment of surprised silence before McBride said quietly, "You mean, you already tried and struck out? Well, I'll be damned! No wonder you're feeling low."

Zach jammed his hand into the pocket of his dinner jacket and muttered, "I feel like pond scum, if you must know."

"Acted like it, too, no doubt. Your problem is, you been alone too long. It's time you moved on, son."

"Maybe it is, but not with her." Moodily, Zach nodded at Claire dancing now with Eric. She outshone every other woman in the room with her elegance and style, and if she wasn't born a princess, she should have been.

"How'd you know?" McBride said. "You ever think to ask her?"

"No. Nor am I about to. We've only known each other a week, for Pete's sake."

"That didn't stop you from jumpin' in the sack with her though, did it? And don't bother answerin' because, from the load of misery on your face, I can figure it out for myself without your drawin' me any pictures. But I'll tell you this: in my day, a man felt obliged to do the right thing by a woman after he'd hung his pants on the back of her bedroom door."

"And too often lived to regret it." He shoved his fingers through his hair irritably. "Use your head, McBride. Even if I was fool enough to ask her if she thought she could settle down here, do you see her being happy with what I've got to offer? Do you see her picking up where Jenny left off?"

"No. And you're even thicker between the ears than I thought if that's what you're expectin' her to do. Because she ain't Jenny, she's herself, and if that's not enough for you, then you're right: you are pond scum and you damn well owe her an explanation for actin' the way you did.''

McBride was right, more than he knew, Zach thought ruefully. If nothing else, she deserved to know why he'd spoken Jenny's name last night when the only woman he should have been thinking about was the one lying with him in the bed.

But trying to catch a moment alone with her was a bit like chasing a butterfly through a summer garden. She flitted from one spot to another, dancing and smiling at any man but him. No matter how determinedly he stalked her, she somehow managed always to wind up on the other side of the room from him.

"Okay, Claire," he muttered, giving up finally and posting himself next to the door again. "We'll play it your way. For now."

Around eleven-thirty, the trio packed it in for the night and people started drifting to the cloakroom for coats and boots before heading outside to the midnight carol service. She left flanked by the Dawsons and Melanie, as if she thought she'd find safety in numbers.

Fine, he thought. *I'm willing to bide my time. But one way or another, Claire, you and I are going to sort things out between us before tonight's over.*

Perhaps if she hadn't found herself so moved by the simple beauty of the chapel in the woods and the midnight service, she would have been more aware of what was going on around her afterward when everyone filed out into the darkness of early Christmas morning. But as it was, she didn't see him standing in the shadow of the double doors until he fell into step beside her.

"There's something I need to tell you," he said, barring her way.

"What, here in this place and at this hour?" she said suspiciously. "Surely not!"

But he was implacable. "Here and now, Claire."

She sighed, making no secret of her impatience. "Now, if you insist, but since we're both going in the same direction anyway, you can talk while we make our way back to the house."

"No. There are too many other people headed that way and I don't want them overhearing. In any case..." He thumbed over his shoulder at the open doors of the chapel and the gleam of candles spilling through the stained glass windows. "I have to close up here before I'm done for the night."

She felt like a sheep singled out from the herd by a wolf. The rest of the congregation was disappearing, those staying in the lodge taking the right fork in the path and those returning to the guest houses taking the left. And none of them looked back to see if she was following.

"Let's go inside," he said, taking her arm. "It's too cold to stand out here. And in case you're wondering, I don't have anything depraved in mind."

"I should think not!" she exclaimed, shrugging him off. "A chapel is hardly the place for seduction."

"I agree."

Perching on the end of the nearest pew, she folded her hands in her lap and looked at him inquiringly, but he seemed in no hurry to continue. "All right, Zachary," she said, when the tension became too much. "I'm here and I'm listening. What is it you want to say that's so urgent it couldn't wait until morning?"

"I want to tell you again how sorry I am about what...happened last night."

"You already did. Repeating yourself—"

"And to explain why I reacted as I did. Because it was

more than just a careless slip of the tongue.'' He stuffed his hands in the pockets of the heavy jacket he wore over his dinner suit and stared moodily at the plain wooden cross hanging on the wall above the cloth-covered table that served as an altar.

At length, he said, ''In a way, it was your fault that it happened at all.''

''*My* fault?'' she echoed indignantly.

''Yes. If you'd been what I expected—''

''And what was that exactly? A more thrilling partner, a better lover?''

''A woman of more…experience.'' As if he couldn't quite bring himself to look her in the eye for what he had to say next, he moved about the chapel and began pinching out the candle flames. ''You can deny it all you like, Claire, but I *am* the first man you've been with and it was that which started me going down a road I'd never thought to travel again. You see, Jenny was a virgin, too.''

''I think she'd no more want you telling me this than I'm interested in hearing it. What goes on between a man and his wife is hardly something to be shared with another woman, and certainly not in a place like this.''

''If she hadn't been a virgin,'' he continued, overriding her objections, ''I would never have married her.''

She felt as if she'd swallowed a lump of ice whole, the cold seeping through her was so intense. ''Of course not,'' she said stonily. ''Men like you do not take other men's leavings.''

''You don't understand,'' he said, reaching up to the tall wooden candlesticks on the altar.

Oh, she understood—all too well! She could be forgiven for not realizing it was possible to fall in love with a man after only a few days, but there was no excuse for her not understanding the price of giving herself to him so easily.

Hadn't she learned years ago that, of all those men her mother had slept with, not one had been willing to offer more than money in exchange for the favor?

She supposed she was lucky Zachary hadn't done the same, but perhaps in Canada it wasn't the custom. Or perhaps, she thought, stifling a sudden urge to giggle hysterically, making love with her was his idea of a Christmas gift.

"What we shared," he continued, apparently determined to rub her nose in the truth, "was something—"

"*Something?*" she cried, the giggles almost dissolving into tears. It had been *everything*! Because she had saved herself for this man. And why? Because she was in love with him, damn it!

"Special," he said.

"No," she said. "Sex is easy and meaningless if all it amounts to is two bodies clinging together for a brief time, then turning away from each other indifferently."

"It was a lot more than that, Claire."

"For you, perhaps, but not for me! Sooner, rather than later, a person is left to face the world poorer for having given something precious of herself to a stranger."

"Don't!" he begged. "Don't belittle yourself or me like that."

But his remorse was too little and came too late. The damage had been done. "You only say that because you feel guilty."

"Yes."

"Well, you're not alone in your misery because I'm full of shame—too full to want to have my actions thrown in my face time and again just to ease your conscience! So let me say this, and then let's please forget what happened between us.

"You are a good man to go to bed with. Quite gentle,

quite considerate. But not, I'm sorry to have to tell you, as experienced or skilled as you might like to think. Without trying to hurt your feelings I have to say I found the whole incident entirely forgettable. Since you clearly feel the same way, let's not burden each other with our regrets now, when it's much too late to change matters. We've shared enough, I think, and if you're the gentleman I like to think you are, you won't persist in reminding me that I was something less than the lady I should have been.''

She was halfway to the door when it suddenly burst open and McBride appeared. ''Oh, shee-oot!'' he exclaimed, stopping short on the threshold. ''Sorry if I'm breakin' up a private conference, Zach, but I noticed light shinin' through the window and thought you'd forgotten to close up.''

''Don't apologize,'' Claire said, brushing by him. ''Zachary and I have said too much already.''

Once outside, she lifted her long skirt clear of her ankles and fled along the lakeshore path. She was gasping by the time she let herself in her front door, as much from the painful clutch of misery inside her as from the frozen air stinging her face. And she had no one to blame but herself.

Of course, she would have to leave Topaz Valley earlier than she'd planned, after all. She'd gambled with every-thing she held dear in the hope of finding love and she'd lost. It was as simple and as complex as that. But to per-petuate the myth that she had emerged untouched from the experience was beyond even her talent for putting on a good front.

For everyone's sake, she somehow managed to keep up appearances on Christmas morning. The only time she came close to losing control was when she suddenly found herself face-to-face with Zachary just after brunch, as people streamed out of the dining room.

For a second or two, they stared at each other with the mutual dismay of ex-lovers who had not parted as friends. But he recovered quickly and pinning a pleasantly impersonal smile on his face, nodded. "Merry Christmas, Claire."

But even those innocuous words wounded her. Had the passion which had touched her so profoundly left him unmoved enough that he could just file it away in the back of his mind like a photograph too unimportant to warrant more than a passing glance, and go on as if nothing had happened?

Sadly, it seemed that it had! Not for him a night of sleepless agonizing such as she'd experienced. Freshly shaven and wearing gray slacks, dark blue sweater and white shirt, he was completely in command of himself and looked disgustingly rested and handsome.

Unable even to drum up the composure to return the empty greeting, she turned away. Another second of looking into his dark and beautiful face, and she'd burst into tears.

Well, enough of such nonsense! She had wept and languished long enough. It was time to take action, to move on with her life. So, while those around her made their way to the lounge, she went in search of someone to help her book a seat on the next flight out of the valley.

Fortunately, even Christmas Day was a working day for the staff who manned the front desk. It took only a few minutes to complete her arrangements. Early on the morning of the twenty-seventh, she would be on her way. In another forty-five hours, Topaz Valley and Zachary Alexander would be in the past.

She found Melanie waiting for her in the lobby. "This

is for Ian,'' she whispered, indicating the package she held. "It's a book that tells all about the history of the resort. Do you think he'll like it?''

"He will treasure it, I'm sure.'' *Just as I will treasure the memory of you, my angel!*

The sudden pang of regret caught Claire unaware and left her teetering again on the brink of tears.

"I wanted to show it to you this morning before I wrapped it up but Dad said I wasn't to come banging on your door ever again unless you invited me over.''

"I'm always happy to see you, Melanie, you know that.''

"You didn't seem all that happy yesterday when you did my hair,'' the girl remarked perceptively. "I guess maybe Dad's right and I have been bugging you too much.''

"I had other things on my mind last night, *chérie,* but if you can spare a few minutes for an old friend, perhaps we can get together later on today? There's something I have to tell you.''

"Okay—if you don't mind waiting till it gets dark, because I'm going skating with Ian again this afternoon.'' Melanie paused, then finished gloomily, "It's his next to last day here, you know. His dad's got to be back in Vancouver by the twenty-eighth.''

Not wishing to spoil the holiday mood, Claire had decided to keep quiet about her own change of plans until after the day's festivities were over, but the realization that she and the Dawsons were leaving together filled her with remorse.

Oh, she had much to answer for—she and Zachary both! To have allowed themselves to become so embroiled in their own pleasures without thought for the repercussions on innocent bystanders like Melanie was unforgivable.

"Then come about half past four,'' she said gently. "I'll

have hot mocha waiting and we'll talk. Also, I have a little something that I'd like to give you in private.''

"Me, too! I mean, I've got a present for you, as well. It's neat how we're both always thinking the same thing, isn't it? As if we've known each other all our lives!''

Melanie's delight, and her smile—so much like her father's—almost destroyed Claire. What right had she to spoil such naive belief that the future held only good things? And yet, what right had she to lie by omission and leave this sweet child to find out for herself that the friend she thought she could trust had suddenly walked out of her life without explanation?

To distract herself from the difficult task ahead, she went cross-country skiing again that afternoon, taking the same route as the day before because she knew she likely would not meet other people and have to pretend a pleasure and enjoyment she wasn't feeling.

In a way, it was her time to come to terms with things, and to say goodbye. In that silent, private place which Melanie had shared with her, she could face the devastation in her heart and begin to accept it.

Leaving her skis propped up against the little railing outside the warming hut, she sat on the steps in the sun and looked out at the scene before her. The ring of snowcapped mountains and the endless stretch of deep blue sky had been here for eons, unmoved by human tragedy, and they would be here long after she was dead. Like love, they would endure.

The thought comforted her because, regardless of what the future held, when she left this place, she would take a little of Melanie with her and of Zachary, too. She would miss them both more than she cared to contemplate but when the need to be with them came over her, she would always be able to take them out of that corner of her heart where she kept the memory of them; of Zachary for being the one to teach her the beauty of two people celebrating passion together, and of Melanie for allowing her to know what it was to love like a mother—unselfishly and without expectation of anything in return but the pleasure of knowing she had made a child happy.

It wasn't as much as she wanted but it was all she was going to get and it would have to be enough.

CHAPTER TEN

SHE'D just finished dressing for dinner when Zachary came banging on her door. At first, she was tempted to ignore him but, "I know you're in there," he bellowed, "and I'll stand out here all night if I have to, so you might as well let me in!"

She had a pretty good idea what had provoked this latest explosion, and let out a weary sigh.

Her meeting with Melanie hadn't been easy. Telling her she was leaving earlier than planned—and the same day as the Dawsons—had produced a flood of dismay which not even Claire's gift of a pretty little antique dress clip had been able to assuage. In an effort to soften the blow, she'd suggested having the girl fly to Vancouver for New Year's Eve, and stay with her in her hotel for a few days. "It'll be up to your father, of course," she'd warned. "But maybe he'll allow it, as long as he knows you're being well looked after."

"Don't count on it," Melanie had said gloomily. "He's such a control freak, he never lets me do anything I want."

Apparently, she'd been right. The way Zachary assaulted the door, so violently that the wood fairly shuddered under the attack, was not the action of a man well pleased with life.

Bracing herself, Claire answered his summons. "I'm not deaf, you know," she said, flinging open the door. "There's no need to behave as if you're storming the Bastille."

Teeth clenched in rage, he said, "If I were, I'd make

sure you remained locked up because, left to roam loose, you're a goddamned menace!''

He hadn't yet finished dressing for the evening. The knife-edge crease in the trousers of his dinner suit hung perfectly above the polished tips of his black shoes but, too fired up with indignation to notice the cold, he hadn't bothered to put on his jacket. The top three studs of his white pleated dress shirt were undone, the cuffs swung loose at his wrists, and his hair draped his brow in disarray. Nevertheless, he was an imposing sight in his wrath.

''I gather I've committed another faux pas,'' she said mildly, noticing the jeweler's box lying on the flat of his hand. ''You don't approve of my gift to your daughter?''

''Where Mel's concerned, I don't approve of a thing you do,'' he snapped. ''She's got no use for expensive trinkets, as anyone with a grain of sense would realize.''

''It's not expensive,'' she said, refusing his attempt to shove the velvet box into her hand. ''The stones aren't real and I won't take it back. I gave it to Melanie and I want her to have it.''

''Too bad. I'm returning it to you anyway.'' The breath hissed from his lungs, an early warning of the eruption to come. ''And that's not all. You've already laid down the law and made it plain you want nothing more to do with me, that nothing I can say or do is going to mend matters between us, and that our whole…*association* has been a mistake. Well now, it's my turn. From here on, you stay away from Mel. No more girl talk, no more little gettogethers, no more filling her head with wacko ideas about flying to Vancouver to play with the rich and not so famous, and no more trying to buy her affections with fancy jewelry. Nothing. *Rien. Comprenez?*''

''I have learned to my cost that you are heartless, Zachary,'' Claire allowed, disgust lending her a fluency not normally at her disposal, "but that you're also a fool comes as a shock. Don't blame me if Melanie defies you, blame yourself for being witless enough to think you can program her wishes to coincide always with yours."

"She's my daughter. I—"

"That doesn't make her one of your assets. She's a human being with needs that exceed anything your stunted imagination can begin to envisage. Unlike you, she can't find emotional nourishment from the ghost of her dead mother. She needs living, human warmth, and I'll continue to offer it to her whether or not you give your permission. I'm leaving here tomorrow but—"

"That's probably the best piece of news I've received all week! The pity of it is, you ever showed up to begin with."

"But your troubles won't leave with me," she continued calmly. "You can doubtless exert your will over Melanie's in this latest fracas but I suggest you enjoy your power while you may. Because eventually she'll take it away from you, and probably much sooner than you realize. Eventually, she *will* choose her own path in life but it's unlikely she will wish to share the adventure with her father. You'll end up solitary, Zachary, a lonely old man with no close ties to anyone, and it will be no less than you deserve."

"At least I'll be rid of you," he said cuttingly. "That'll make up for a lot!"

"But you'll never be entirely rid of me, Zachary, because I'll leave Melanie my friendship and love."

"In exchange for what?" he jeered.

"For nothing but the satisfaction of knowing that, if she ever needs help or refuge, she can call on me."

"Don't hold your breath," he said. "Mel likes to make out she's a misunderstood waif desperate for a sympathetic ear, but it's all an act. I hate to be the one to break it to you, but with a kid her age, out of sight means out of mind. I guarantee she'll have forgotten your name before the new year rolls in.''

''Don't count on it,'' Claire said, though she almost wished he was right. At least then, she wouldn't have to bear the burden of knowing she'd added to the child's unhappiness. ''Melanie's past the age where you can assume that she'll abide by your rules just because you say she must.''

She spoke in the heat of the moment, more as a gesture of her own defiance than anything else, and never dreaming how soon the prediction would come back to haunt her.

The morning of the twenty-seventh began with guests being warned of a storm expected to sweep into the area by mid afternoon. ''Enjoy the sun while it lasts,'' one of the ski instructors told them, ''and those of you planning to leave by helicopter please be ready for departure immediately after lunch.''

At ten o'clock, a busload of guests left for the long drive to Vancouver, hoping to clear the area before the clouds rolled in. Horrified at the thought of being held hostage by the weather, Claire spent the morning in the library and prayed that conditions would hold long enough for the helicopter to be able to fly its passengers out of the valley.

The preceding two days had been difficult enough and she truly didn't think she could survive another night under the same roof with Zachary. Even though there was no connecting door between his part of the house and hers, the walls just weren't thick enough to shut him out.

Awake or asleep, she was aware of him just a few feet away. She knew when he came in and when he went out. She heard the sound of water running when he took a shower, she heard the muted rumble of his voice when he answered his telephone.

To make matters worse, Melanie had been sullen and withdrawn except for those times when she was weeping. "I hate you!" Claire had heard her rage at her father, just the night before. "I wish I was dead and I bet you wish I was, too!"

Already bruised beyond bearing, Claire's heart had bled for both of them. She ached to cross the short stretch of no-man's-land between her front door and theirs, and to implore them to treasure the bond between them because it deserved better than to be subjected to such abuse.

But she knew doing so would merely incense Zachary further. Not that he'd been outwardly unpleasant since their last confrontation on Christmas Day. On the contrary, he'd been faultlessly polite, coldly charming and so utterly remote that she might have been just another face in the crowd for all the emotion he betrayed when he looked at her.

Looked at her? Looked *through* her was a more apt description! She had become a nonperson. He had predicted that Melanie would have forgotten the name Claire Durocher by New Year's Day, but he hadn't waited even that long to wipe his memory clean of it.

She could only hope he wouldn't feel compelled to go through the formalities of saying goodbye. She, who prided herself on having learned to hold her head high and face whatever had to be faced without flinching, wanted only to slink away unnoticed.

Even that small concession was denied her, though. She was on her way to lunch when the Dawsons returned from one last ski run. At the same time, Zachary appeared from the office behind the front desk and short of turning tail and running back the way she'd come, there was no way Claire could avoid any of them.

Ignoring her, Zachary nodded pleasantly at Ian. "So, did you and Mel have a good morning?"

The boy looked puzzled. "Melanie wasn't with us, sir."

"Oh? She told me she would be."

"Because of the weather warning, we decided to stick to the runs closest to the resort, rather than risk missing our flight out this afternoon," Paul Dawson explained. "When we told Melanie, she decided not to join us."

"She said she wanted to ski the back bowl," Ian said.

"Alone? She knows better than to do that. And she knows better than to show up late, no matter where she's been or who she's with." Although Zachary sounded annoyed, his eyes betrayed sudden anxiety and, as though to add credence to his concern, the bright shadows outside blurred and faded as the sun slid behind a layer of cloud advancing from the north.

"Maybe," Claire said, sympathetic alarm taking precedence over her wish to avoid further discourse with the man, "she's with her uncle."

But Eric came into the lobby just in time to dash that hope. "I haven't seen her," he said. "I spent the morning skiing Powder Peak. Why? Is something wrong?"

"I hope not." But Zachary's face said otherwise. Claire hadn't thought ever to see him frightened. Until that moment, he had seemed invincible. Now fear carved his features, compressing his lips into a thin line that pulled the skin even more tautly over his cheekbones. "But the fact that she's not here…"

He left the sentence unfinished because, even though they all knew the direction his thoughts were taking, to air the words aloud would have been to give them unholy power. Melanie could not be lost on the mountain with a storm approaching. It was unthinkable.

"Could she be at home?" Claire suggested, casting about for a more acceptable alternative.

"And miss a meal? You've got to be kidding!"

Stung by his withering tone and the way he flicked his gaze over her as if he thought a drunken field mouse could have come up with a more worthwhile suggestion, Claire said sharply, "Perhaps the prospect of having to say good-bye to people she cares about robbed her of her appetite. Or perhaps she's not feeling well. I don't pretend to know for sure but, if it were my child missing, I wouldn't be so quick to dismiss any idea until I'd looked into it."

For a moment, he stared at her, his resentment almost palpable. Then he stabbed a thumb toward the open door of the dining room. "Get started on lunch while I take a run back to the house. The way the weather's closing in, you won't want to keep that helicopter waiting."

Only a man with antifreeze in his veins would seriously expect her to show any interest in food with Melanie gone missing! Passing by the selection of hot dishes on the buffet, she poured herself a cup of coffee and perched on a chair near the door to await his return.

He was back at the lodge within five minutes, fear a living thing crawling through his gut. He'd found no sign of Mel at the house except for her dirty cereal bowl on the kitchen counter and her cross-country ski boots at the back door.

McBride, who'd obviously heard the news, approached him. "Any clue as to where the lass might be, Zach?"

"Uh-uh." He shook his head and looked out at the slab of cloud creeping across the sky. "I'm worried, McBride. The way the weather's blowing in, we'll be lucky if visibility holds out for more than a couple of hours and I don't need to tell you what her chances are if we don't find her before dark. Round up the ski patrol and have them meet me in the office ASAP.''

He strode away, unaware that he was not alone. Only when she raised a hand to stop him from shutting the office door in her face did he realize that Claire had followed him.

"What the hell do you want?" he barked.

"To help, Zachary," she said.

He curled his lip. "You've done enough damage as it is. Your kind of help I can do without."

"No, you can't," she said. "Nor can you allow your pride to blind you to the gravity of what's happened. That's a big mountain out there and you need as many volunteers as possible to join in the search for Melanie. I'm a strong and capable skier and whatever else you think of me, you know that to be true. So let me help."

"No. I want you on that chopper and on your way out of my life. I wish I'd never set eyes on you. Mel and I were doing fine until you showed up and started putting ideas in her head. And now...and now..."

For one god-awful minute, he choked up and the fear, taking advantage of his weakness, grabbed a firmer hold. *I wish I was dead,* Mel had said. Had she meant it? Would she deliberately try to—?

He slammed the office door back on its hinges so hard that it bounced off the wall, and refused to allow himself to complete the thought.

The cause of all his troubles stood quietly watching. "Get out of my sight," he said thickly. "Go paint your toenails or something until it's time for you to leave. I've got work to do."

"I'm not leaving," she said.

He swiveled a glare her way. "Yes, you are, lady. You're leaving, all right."

"I am not!" she cried, planting her fists on her hips. "What kind of person do you think I am that I could walk away from here without knowing first that Melanie is safe?"

"You're trouble," he spat. "If it weren't for your meddling in matters that are none of your business, my little girl wouldn't now be somewhere out there on that mountain with a storm threatening her safety and that of everyone going out to look for her."

At his words, her eyes grew round as saucers and the color leached from her heart-shaped face until she was as pale as old bones left out too long in the sun. "No, Zachary!" she practically whimpered, sinking onto the nearest chair. "I surely didn't do such a thing!"

For a moment, he felt remorse. But his own fear, masked in anger, was stronger. Revved up on righteous indignation, he continued his tirade. "Yes, you did," he said viciously. "Can you handle the fact that you've probably sent her to an early grave, Claire? Does that satisfy your insatiable need to undermine my authority by encouraging her to defy me? Does it make you feel good to know you wield such power?"

McBride arrived on the scene just then, thank God, or there was no telling what he might have said or done next. "Take it easy, son," he muttered, clamping a hand on his shoulder. "You ain't doin' anybody any good with that kind of talk."

Cursing, Zach turned away from the sight of Claire trembling in the chair, and spread a large map out on the desk. "What's taking people so long? It's time we got this show on the road."

Just as McBride left to ferry passengers to the helipad,

the ski patrol showed up, split into groups, organized the equipment they'd need, the routes they'd take, the frequency with which they'd check in by radio. And after a lot of argument, they persuaded him to stay behind and man the control center. "You can't be everywhere at once," they told him. "It's better that you're here. That way, you'll know right away when we find her."

When, they said. Not *if.* And for that he thanked them, albeit silently, in the anguished mess that was his heart.

"Just get to her before nightfall," he said, holding himself together by sheer willpower because everything else about him—his bones, his muscles, his brain—was coming unstrung. He couldn't do this again. He couldn't bury another member of his family.

They left, their eyes full of sympathy—and worse, pity. And he was suddenly alone with the empty silence and a host of memories he couldn't bear to face. *You never let me do anything I want! How come you always have to decide what's best for me, Dad? Why can't I be like other kids and just have a normal life?*

"Come home again, Mel, and you can have the moon," he whispered, burying his face in his hands.

A hand came down on his shoulder, heavy and comforting. "You ain't givin' up on me, are you, Zach?" McBride asked huskily.

He lifted his head and blinked. "I thought you were supposed to be driving the chopper passengers up to the helipad."

"I did. They're safely on their way, son."

"She didn't give you grief about leaving—Claire, I mean?"

McBride's eyebrows almost disappeared into his hairline. "She ain't gone, leastways not that way. She's out lookin' for Mel. I thought you knew that."

She would be, Zach thought wearily. When had she ever paid a blind bit of attention to anything he had to say?

Someone brought him coffee, a sandwich.

There were no windows in the office and when the waiting got to be too much, he paced the foyer from one set of doors to the next, and gazed out at the thickening gloom. By two-thirty, the mountain peaks were buried in mist as thick as oatmeal. By three, the far side of the lake had disappeared. Shortly after, the snow started.

Periodically, the search teams called in to report on the ground covered. They'd found no sign of Mel.

At four, he became aware of laughter and music as guests gathered in the lounge for an early cocktail hour. He supposed he should be glad they hadn't noticed anything was wrong. It wasn't good for business when somebody went missing from a luxury resort.

Especially if it was his child.

He wasn't a praying man but, as the minutes crawled by, he was ready to sell his soul if that was the price God demanded to bring her home safely.

Just before five, the search parties began straggling back. Without daylight, their task was impossible. At exactly seven forty-three, with all of them huddled over the map to decide where to start things up again the next morning, the front desk put through a call from the Vancouver City Police headquarters.

"We've picked up a girl of about fourteen," an Officer Paley told Zach. "Her only ID is a Topaz Valley Resort ski pass bearing her name and picture. Melanie Alexander; dark hair, blue eyes, about five three. Are you missing anyone fitting that description?"

Zach felt as if his heart had dropped through the soles of his feet and hit the floor. The coffee he'd consumed roiled in his stomach so violently he thought he was going to be ill.

"Yes," he managed to croak, as unprepared for this call as he had been the last time he'd picked up the phone and had a faceless police official ask him if he recognized a name and description. The only difference was, this time it was Mel and not Jenny who was the subject in question.

"Claims she's your daughter," the officer went on.

"She did?" He swallowed the mud rising in his throat and forced out his next words. "You mean, she's…?"

"She's fine, Mr. Alexander. Scared but otherwise okay."

The sweat sprang from every pore in his body. "How—where—?"

"We got called to the Waterfront Hotel about half an hour ago. Apparently the girl came in on a bus charter from your neck of the woods expecting to meet a Miss Claire Durocher who was supposed to have checked in here around four this afternoon. But the lady didn't show up and hasn't been heard from."

Claire, again. Everything always came back to Claire! "No," he said, relief leaving him light-headed. "She missed her flight out and is still here. She—*we* won't be arriving until late tomorrow morning at the earliest."

"Is there anyone else we can turn your daughter over to until then? A relative, or family friends?"

Only Eric, and he wasn't home. He'd spent the afternoon combing the mountain, looking for his niece. As for friends…

The accusations echoed through his mind. *I never meet anyone my own age, stuck away up here…you treat me as if I'm still five years old and too dumb to know what I want.…*

Okay, Mel, he thought. You want to prove you're old enough to take some responsibility for yourself, here's your chance. "I'm afraid not," he told the police officer, "but if you can arrange for a dependable member of the hotel staff to stay with her overnight and see she has everything she needs, I think that'll take care of things until we get there. And while you're doing that, I'd like to speak to my daughter."

She came on the line and tried putting on a brave front, but he knew the day had taken a toll she wouldn't soon forget. She'd discovered that running away didn't solve a thing. But at thirteen, she couldn't have been expected to know any better, whereas he had no such excuse. Thank God it wasn't too late to make up for lost time!

Hanging up the phone finally, he looked at the grinning faces surrounding him. "Go celebrate," he said, "she's safe and you've all earned a five-star dinner. And tonight the drinks are on me."

Suspiciously red around the eyes, McBride blew his nose and asked, "You comin' to join us, son?"

"Not right now."

Right now, there was only one person he wanted to be with. He wanted Claire. He wanted to wrap his arms around her and tell her he was a bloody fool. He wanted to tell her that she had more generosity in her little finger than he had in his entire being, and that he was sorry he'd been too mean-spirited to see it before. Damn it, he wanted someone to cry with.

"By the way, where's Claire?" he said.

He knew from the sudden silence, the blank looks, and the way his built-in radar made the hair on the back of his neck rise up as if he'd touched a live wire, that as one nightmare ended, another was beginning.

"She detoured by way of the warming hut on Chimney Ridge when we headed back down the hill," somebody volunteered. "Said she had an idea Mel might have holed up there and that she'd make her own way back to the bottom of the hill after she'd checked it out.''

''And you let her go, knowing she's unfamiliar with the terrain? Good God, where were your brains?''

''There was no stopping her, Zach. She felt it was her fault Mel had gone missing and said she couldn't face you again until she'd found her.''

''You've been back nearly three hours.'' He heard his voice veering out of control and didn't care. ''For crying out loud, why have you waited until now to tell me this?''

They shuffled their feet and looked anywhere but at him. ''I guess we figured she'd already checked in,'' one of them finally said. ''It never occurred to us she was still out there. You want us to go looking for her?''

He shook his head, knowing they weren't at fault. In her own way, Claire was every bit as stubborn as he was. Once she'd made up her mind to pass by the Chimney Ridge hut, there'd have been no talking her out of it.

Nor was he blameless. He'd railed at her, accused her, condemned her. If anyone had driven her to rash action, he had. And if anyone was to risk his neck finding her, it was he.

CHAPTER ELEVEN

IN DAYLIGHT and given half-decent conditions, he could have made it to the hut in forty minutes. But even though he knew the route well, it took him nearly an hour and a half to reach the Chimney Ridge plateau in the dark.

The blood was thundering in his ears as he topped the last rise—less from the exertion of the climb than from dread. He hardly dared look toward the hut. The nightmare possibilities of where Claire might be, of what might have happened to her if she weren't there, had dogged him every step of the way.

Now, faced with the answer, he suddenly wanted to postpone the moment of truth indefinitely. Not knowing anything was preferable to discovering the worst.

Time, though, was very much of the essence. Slipping his backpack to the ground, he reached up to turn off the lamp strapped to his helmet and peered intently into the thinning mist swirling around him. The dark bulk of the hut rose out of the snow some twenty feet ahead and...

Hallelujah! A square of pale light shone feebly at the window, the kind made by a candle or perhaps an oil lamp turned low. Removing his skis, he planted them tips up in the snow, slung his poles over them and with his backpack swinging from one hand, approached the hut and opened the door.

At first he saw only the wood stove, a can of soup heating on its top and the flames licking around the logs stuffed in its cast-iron belly throwing out a yellow glow. Then, as his vision adjusted to the shadows, he found her.

Covered by a green sleeping bag, she lay on one of the narrow cots which she'd dragged close enough to the stove for the firelight to glimmer darkly on her hair spread over the striped ticking of the mattress.

Squatting down beside her, he gazed at her sleeping face. Noted the smudges of exhaustion beneath her eyes which not even the thick, silky crescents of her lashes could hide. Placed two fingers at the pulse spot just below the corner of her jaw and watched the even rise and fall of her chest. Satisfied that her breathing was normal, he lifted the sleeping bag to feel her fingers and narrow, elegant feet, and found them comfortably warm.

Only then did he allow the trapped air in his lungs to escape. It trembled over her face, stirring little wisps of hair at her forehead. As if aware of his scrutiny, she sighed in her sleep and the corners of her mouth lifted slightly in a smile.

That mouth...! Leaning closer, he studied the full rich curve of her lips, the feature which most betrayed her zest for life, for love. A cupid's bow of a mouth, and well named at that, quick to laugh, to tease with a smile, and quicker still to bloom with passion beneath his.

He wanted to know that passion again, to hold her close to his heart and hear her cry out his name in ecstasy. He wanted to wipe away her tears afterward and tell her that she was perfect, that she made him feel like a king. He never wanted any other man to know her, to love her, as he did.

As he did...!

The revelation stunned him. Numbly, he waited for the aftershock to hit, for the reasoning part of his mind to scoff at the idea. For words like "ludicrous," "juvenile," "infatuation" and "lust" to spearhead a rebuttal. Instead, he was filled with such shocking certainty that it left him weak in the knees.

Good God, he'd done everything in his power to drive her away. Insulted her, belittled her, accused her. If she had died on this mountain, he would have been to blame. *It's your fault my little girl's missing,* he'd railed at her. *Does it make you feel good to know you've probably sent her to her death?*

Almost blinded by guilt and remorse, he dipped his head and kissed her, softly, achingly. And like the sleeping beauty she was, she opened her eyes at his touch and looked at him.

"Zachary?" she murmured fuzzily. "Is it really you?"

"Yes," he said, his voice thick with emotion. "Who else were you expecting?"

Of course, she was dreaming. Had been dreaming for days now, and too often waking up disappointed. Which was why she tried to pull the covers more snugly around herself and sink back into sleep. Because this time, she would not let the dream end. Reality was cold and cruel, and she far from ready to face it.

"Open your eyes, Claire," he said, his voice seeming to fold her in warm black satin. "Time to wake up."

"Non," she whimpered—another sign she was dreaming. She never whimpered! "Not yet."

"Sweetheart," he said tenderly, "you have to talk to me. I need to know that you're really okay."

Sweetheart… She smiled and burrowed luxuriously under the thick cover. Such a dream should never end!

"We've found Mel," he said.

His words pierced the bubble of fantasy and brought the

day's events rushing back. She shot upright and stared at him.

"Easy, sweetheart," he said, pressing her back against the lumpy, ugly mattress. "It's okay. *She's* okay. You're the one I'm worried about now."

"How—where did you find her? Why did she—?"

"All that can wait," he said. "Right now, I want to make sure you're not hurt."

Pulling aside the sleeping bag, he ran deft hands over her limbs, her shoulders, her neck, searching for possible injuries. She lay there and let him, reveling in his touch, in the warm probing of his lean, capable fingers.

At last satisfied, he sat back on his heels and regarded her sternly. "Splitting off from the search party was a damn fool thing to do. This is alpine wilderness, not some suburban ski hill. You're lucky you didn't wind up dead at the bottom of a crevasse with a broken neck. You know that, don't you?"

"But—" she began.

"And what would I have done then?" No longer soothing, his voice assumed a dangerous edge. "Did you stop to think about that? Do you *ever* stop to think before you fling yourself headlong into whatever impulse strikes your fancy?"

"I was—"

"I've already got my hands full with Mel. I don't need more gray hairs. I don't need you—"

"I know that," she said indignantly, stopping him in mid flow. "You've made it clear enough that you'll *never* need me."

"Damn right!" he raged. "I'd have to be mad to hook myself up with a woman as willful as a mule. Look at what you do to me! Nobody else brings out the worst in me the way you do! So help me, Claire, if I had the last ten days to live over again, I'd..."

But she stopped listening because she saw suddenly what he would not acknowledge in words: the pain that filled his eyes, the fear he'd never admit to, the vulnerability he tried so hard to suppress. She saw the grooves beside his mouth, put there by worry. She saw the fatigue that left his features drawn and pale. But he would not give in to such weaknesses. Instead, he tried to impose the same iron discipline on his emotions that he brought to bear on every other part of his life.

When he finally wound down into exhausted silence, she put her hand against his cheek and said, "Such a barking dog you are! So much noise, and so little bite! I'm not the only one who is stubble, Zachary. You're stubble, too."

"Huh?" He stared at her as if he wasn't sure which of them could lay closer claim to madness. "What the hell are you talking about?"

"Us," she said softly. "We are more alike than you want to know, *mon amour*. Both of us stubble as mules."

"Stubborn," he said, sounding dazed. "You mean 'stubborn.' And damn it, stop trying to derail things by mangling the language again." He drew in a determined breath and started over, once more in charge of himself and the world. "You and I are not leaving here until we come to an understanding. I will not—*will* not—tolerate your endangering yourself and others just because you...damn it, stop looking at me like that. Stop it, I said! Making your eyes all big and innocent won't work. You know damned well that I'm right, just as you know...oh, hell...!"

She'd thought the only way she'd know his kiss again would be in her dreams. Had, indeed, tried to immortalize the last time he'd held her so close and devoured her with such hunger, because she'd believed it would have to last her a lifetime. But even recent memory was but a pale counterfeit, incapable of reproducing the splendor of the real thing.

The urgent, seeking way he sealed his mouth to hers undid her. How was it possible that, with just a touch, he could cause her heart to seize up with pleasure and her stomach to fold in on itself? Yet, with that kiss, he enslaved her all over again, drawing the very soul from her, and reducing her to a molten heap of helpless surrender willing to abide by whatever edict he next ordained.

When they were both gasping for breath, he drew her into a sitting position on the cot, crushed her against him, heartbeat to heartbeat, and said brokenly, "I was afraid I had killed you, Claire."

"*Non*, Zachary," she whispered against his mouth. "I'm a survivor. You're not going to get rid of me quite so easily."

He thrust his fingers through her hair, molded his hands to her skull, feathered kisses light as snowflakes over her eyelids and across her cheek to her ear. And with every touch, each muttered endearment, he told her that he wanted her—probably not forever, alas, but here and now, in this spartan little hut on the side of a mountain in the middle of a winter storm, with nothing but the barest essentials to set the scene.

And because she loved him, she gave to him, winding her arms around his neck and taking him with her as she sank back down to the mattress. Never mind that, in doing so, she was inviting further hurt tomorrow, when his world was set right again and she had served her purpose. Tonight, he needed her and she would not turn away from him.

They wore so many clothes, though, and that was what caused the trouble. If she'd taken off her ski suit before falling asleep, if he'd removed his jacket and boots before awaking her, they could so quickly and easily have stripped away what remained and made love.

Even with all those layers of wool and cotton impeding them, his touch left her sleek and aching for him. "Zachary," she whispered, plucking feverishly at his sweater to find the smooth, hard planes of his bare chest buried underneath, and tilting her hips to nest against his.

But, "No," he said, rolling away from her. "Not like this. Not a second time."

"Why not?" She was whimpering again. Bereft, stripped of pride, and filled with a great gnawing emptiness.

"Because," he said, "making love should be about two people. And the last time—your first time—it was all about me. I gave you nothing."

"It's what I can give *you* that matters, *mon amour*," she murmured, and reached out to lay her palm against the proud swell of his flesh beneath the snug-fitting ski pants.

He might have capitulated then. She saw the tortured glitter in his eyes, heard the agony of his indrawn breath, felt the tremor that shook him. But then another sound intruded, a metallic rattling followed by a sputtering hiss.

"Damnation!" he exclaimed, springing toward the stove too late to stop the can of soup from exploding and sending streams of hot broth spurting in all directions.

Well, it was enough to put everything else off the boil! By the time he'd wrapped the can in a piece of toweling and flung it out into the snow, making love to her was the last thing on his mind. "I hope you hadn't set your heart on having that for dinner," he remarked, coming back into the hut and shoving the door closed.

"No," she said sadly, knowing that the moment had fled and that there was no recalling the magic which, too briefly, had been theirs. "I can see that you're anxious to get back to the lodge."

He stared at her in amazement. "Are you kidding? Claire, I took my life in my hands to find you. Now that I have—found you, that is—I don't propose risking your neck or mine just for the sake of sleeping in my own bed tonight."

"But what about Melanie? Who'll look after her?"

"She's in good hands," he assured her. "Staying in your Vancouver hotel suite, as a matter of fact, chaperoned by a nice, grandmotherly housekeeper, while you and I make do with somewhat less comfortable surroundings."

"I wouldn't trade this place for all the palaces in Europe," she said. "Right here, with you, is exactly where I want to be."

He hauled his knapsack onto the mattress and tipped out the contents. "Nice of you to say so, sweetheart," he said, a rare and tender humor in his tone, "but knowing that the supplies in these huts are pretty basic, I had the foresight to bring a few goodies to see us through the night."

He tossed aside a first aid kit in favor of a round metal can and a pewter hip flask. "We don't need that, thank God, but we can use these. Coffee and cognac would go down rather well with a sandwich right now, wouldn't you say?"

"I suppose," she said, sounding less than enthusiastic.

He looked at her in surprise. "What's wrong? Aren't you hungry?"

"Yes," she heard herself say shockingly. "But not for food. We were about to make love, Zachary. How can you behave as if we weren't? Am I of so little consequence to you?"

The coffee and cognac forgotten, he pulled her close again. "I wish you were," he said. "Then I could ignore my conscience and pick up where we just left off. But the truth is, I should never have started making love to you at all."

"Why did you, then?"

"Because I was so relieved at finding you alive and all in one piece that I wasn't thinking straight."

"And now you are?"

"Yes." He put her from him and took down a couple of thick white plates and cups from a shelf next to the stove. "And before matters get out of hand again, we need to talk. About a lot of things. About where we go from here and whether or not the feelings we have for one another amount to something more than mistletoe madness."

"I thought you had already decided that they don't," she said, watching as he sliced bread and cheese and cold meat with a Swiss Army knife and filled a plate for her. "You told me to go back where I came from and to leave you in peace."

"I said a lot of things I didn't mean and it's not to my credit that it took two near-tragedies to make me admit it, but I'm done with backing away from the truth."

As though determined to leave her on tenterhooks for as long as possible, he stopped talking while he went to the door and filled an ancient enameled pot with snow, threw in several scoops of ground coffee, and put it to boil on the stove.

"The problem with our relationship," he finally continued, "is that we started at the end instead of the beginning, and that was a mistake. So, before we wind up making a colossal mess of something which I'm beginning to believe might be worth saving, let's go back and cover a few preliminaries. I'm more than Mel's father and the owner-operator of a fancy resort, and I'm damn sure there's more to Claire Durocher than meets the eye. We might not have known each other very long, sweetheart, but before tomorrow comes, I intend for us to know each other very well.''

If he had his way, it would be the end of everything, Claire realized hopelessly. He was a man grounded in reality, blunt almost to a fault and not inclined to tolerate dishonesty in others. Once he learned she was living a lie, he would walk away from her. ''I don't think sharing our life histories is going to change anything, Zachary. I already know what kind of woman you want and I am not she.''

''You mean you're not like Jenny,'' he said, stirring the coffee with the handle of a long wooden spoon. ''That doesn't necessarily mean you're not the kind of woman I want.''

''Of course it does! You loved her enough to marry her, to have a child by her.''

''I married her because I got her pregnant, Claire, not because I loved her.''

''How can that be?'' she cried. ''You told me—on Christmas Eve in the chapel, you told me—that you married her because she was a virgin. Are you saying now that you lied to me, there in that holy place?''

''You weren't listening to me that night, Claire. In fact, if you recall, you refused to let me finish what I was trying to tell you. But there's no running away from me now. You're going to hear the whole story whether you want to or not. And just to set the record straight, I didn't say that Jenny was a virgin when I married her. I said that she was a virgin when I met her, and that was why I married her. There's a subtle difference there that I think you missed.''

''You're talking in riddles,'' she cried, more confused by the minute.

''For once in your life, shut up and listen, darling,'' he said in a tone that left her damp with wanting him. ''Jenny was an innocent who, though not a blue blood like you, came from a solidly respectable middle-class family. She was a nice, well-brought-up girl whom I seduced into forgetting the values she'd been taught to honor and when she told me there was a baby on the way, I could no more have turned away from her than I could have denied it was my child she was carrying.''

She was all the things I'm not and never will be, Claire thought, a rush of despair overshadowing her desire. *If he couldn't love her, how could he ever love me?*

"Why did my trying to explain that to you on Christmas Eve upset you so?" he asked, watching her closely.

"It shouldn't have," she said dully. "But when you said you married her because she was a virgin, I thought what you were telling me was that you couldn't take seriously a woman like me, who would give herself to a man outside of marriage.''

"The spoken word has been a problem for us from the word go," he said, the glimmer of a smile relieving his sober expression. "I can see that, in future, I'm going to have to think twice before I open my mouth.''

In future? There could be no future for the two of them, she knew that. Quickly, before her heart could delude her into believing otherwise, she said, "You might have married her because there was a baby to think of, but you were happy with her nonetheless.''

"In time, I was. Things didn't start out that way, though. She was ready to settle down but it was the furthest thing from my mind. When I found out she was pregnant, I took the moral high ground and married her but not, I'm ashamed to say, because I was in love with her.''

"Yet your marriage endured.''

"Yes. And you want to know why? Because she loved enough for both of us. She guessed how I felt, but she kept on loving me anyway.'' Mystified, he shook his head. ''I don't know, maybe hers was the sort of selflessness only a woman's capable of, because I see the same quality in you, in your sweetness and generosity with Mel.''

But there's a difference between us, mon amour. Unlike her, I want to take, as well as give. ''She must have been a very special lady.''

''She was. We started out living in a miserable basement suite in Vancouver and had almost no money but she never once complained.''

''And eventually, you came to see that you had found a treasure in her.'' Claire could see in his eyes that it was so. In time, he had come to love his Jenny because she was honest and good and real.

''Yes. She brought a stability to my life and we had some good years before it all came to an end, but we were never...'' He hunched his shoulders, searching for the right word. ''...delirious together. She knew it and never asked for more than I could give. And I learned to live with the guilt of my omission because I never expected to find myself single again, or obsessed by another woman in a way that I was never drawn to her. And then I met you, and suddenly, all hell broke loose.''

As though he couldn't quite bring himself to follow through on that admission, he paced to the stove and peered at the coffee. ''I think this is about ready to pour. Shall we spike it with a shot of brandy?''

''If you like. Is it still snowing?''

''No. The cloud was lifting when I came up here. The storm will have blown over by morning.''

He cleared his throat and stared into his cup, uneasy, she could see, both with himself and his feelings, and with her. Finally, with his back to her, he picked up his story again. ''Until you came along, I don't think I realized how much

I'd cheated Jenny. I never told her I loved her when we were…together, when reserve is at its weakest and passion rips the truth out of a man. And yet, with you who were as wrong for me as she was right, I was ready to bare my soul. It terrified me, Claire, and it shamed me because I found myself wanting to give to a stranger something I'd never been able to give to my wife. And that's why…''

Again, he cleared his throat and flung her a hunted look over his shoulder. ''Is any of this making any sense at all?''

''Yes,'' she said sadly. ''That's why you apologized to her when you had been intimate with me. I see that now, Zachary, and I'm sorry, too—sorry for not showing more understanding, but even more sorry that you were right in saying that I'm all wrong for you, because it's true. I am not the woman for you.''

''Forget what I said before! That was just the idiot in me trying to talk his way out of a situation he was too scared to confront. The truth is, I'm in love with you, and I can't just let you walk out of my life.''

''Yes, you can,'' she said, her throat aching. ''Because I'm not exactly the person you think I am. I have secrets, Zachary. Shameful secrets.''

He swung back to face her at that. ''What are you trying to tell me?'' he asked sharply. ''That you're married to some rich old aristocrat too decrepit to make love to you, so you decided to have a fling with me to find out what you were missing?''

''I'm not married, nor do I have blood connections with European royalty. I have money, yes, but I'm no heiress. Except for a small inheritance from a very dear old friend, I earned what I have through my own efforts. My jewels are not real, I wasn't born with a silver spoon in my mouth, and I didn't go to a fine finishing school for young ladies.''

"If that's supposed to make me change my mind about you, I'm afraid it isn't working."

"Then perhaps this will," she said. "My mother was a prostitute."

He looked both startled and shocked. "That's a bit strong, surely? You mean she had lovers."

"No. This isn't one of those times that I'm not sure if I've found the right word, Zachary. My mother sold herself to any man willing to pay her asking price. I grew up in the slums of Marseilles and have no idea who my father was. I doubt that my mother knew, either. As a child, I often went to bed hungry and walked the streets in rags."

"But you never sold yourself," he said, coming to sit beside her on the cot and tipping up her chin so that she had to meet his gaze. "I know you never did that, Claire. I'm the first and only man to make love to you."

"No, I didn't sink to that level. Instead, I went through rich people's garbage bins and stole things they no longer wanted but which I thought I could sell at the street markets. Broken beads which I mended with cotton thread, shoes no longer considered haute couture, bits of silk which I sewed into scarves and handkerchiefs; buttons and buckles which I clipped from cast-off clothes—anything which would bring in money enough to buy bread and a little cheese and a few pieces of fruit too bruised for others to want."

"Good God!" he exclaimed in a hushed tone. "How old were you when you started this?"

"Nine, ten—I don't remember exactly. But old enough to know what it was like to have nothing, no one. Old enough to know that the reason I had to wait outside in the night was that my mother didn't want her clientele to know that she had a child. And old enough to recognize the smell of cheap wine on her breath when she at last opened the door and let me in.''

He looked away from her at that, and wiped a hand over his face as if to erase the image she'd created. As if, by association, he'd picked up the dirt from which she'd sprung. And why wouldn't he? Why would a decent man like him want to have a woman like her at his side?

"Was there no one who cared about you?" he asked at last, in a low voice.

"Yes. There was an older woman who had a stall at the market and whom I met when I was twelve. Her name was Belle and she taught me all about paste jewelry. In those days, there was not much demand for it but she was clever and saw its value. She taught me how to tell the difference between good quality antique reproductions and cheap imitations. That might sound like a contraction of terms—''

"Not contraction," he said gently. "A contradiction of terms."

"*Merci*. But I think you know what I mean. There is faux and there is cheap, and they're not necessarily the same. I am faux, Zachary, but I've never been cheap. Belle taught me that, too. She said that if I didn't value myself highly, no one else would."

"She was right."

"*Oui*. I loved her, you know. She was the real mother in my life and oh, Zachary, I needed a mother so! When she died, I was more heartbroken than when I buried the woman who had given birth to me. And only after Belle, too, was dead did I discover how much she had loved me. She left me everything—her collection of paste, her expertise and more money than I knew existed in the world. I'd believed her to be a simple woman of modest means but she had saved and invested wisely. And she gave it all to me with only one condition: that I go to school and learn all a woman has to know to pass for a lady in high society. Which I did within the year, when I was eighteen.''

He said nothing. He simply stared at her. He looked like a man who had woken up from a coma and didn't know who he was anymore. She sipped her coffee and nibbled on a piece of cheese, to give him time to assimilate what she'd told him. Now that her truth was out, she felt strangely calm.

At length he got up and fed more wood into the stove. "And then?" he said, content to remain as far away from her as the confines of the small hut would allow, now that she'd revealed herself as the daughter of a whore.

"I opened a little shop in the best part of the city. But because I couldn't bring myself to sell the lovely things Belle had left to me, I...how do you say it?...rented her jewelry instead.''

"You *rented* it?''

"*Oui*. Any time there was an important society event— a party for visiting royalty, a charity ball, a film festival— any sort of affair where women want to dazzle and look their best, they came to me and, for a price, they borrowed my faux gems. And whenever the opportunity came my way, I bought more items, thereby adding to my collection without ever diminishing it. Like you, I'm an entrepreneur, wouldn't you say?''

"To put it mildly! What do you call this shop of yours?''

"Shops," she corrected him. "Eventually, I opened another boutique in Marseilles then, when that, too, became a success, others in Paris, Rome, New York, and San Francisco. And they all have the same name, Belles Illusions. I'm thinking of opening one in Vancouver next, which is one reason I chose to spend Christmas here, so that I could throw stones at two birds at the same time.''

"You mean, kill two birds with—oh, hell, never mind

what you mean!'' He shook his head the way a dog might shake water from its fur. ''More to the point, how many people know the real Claire Durocher—assuming that's your real name?''

''It is. Only the outer trappings are false. But as far as others are concerned, no one knows my story, except for you.''

''I see.'' He refilled his cup, adding a generous splash of cognac to the coffee then, whistling tunelessly, sauntered to the window and stared out.

She watched. She waited. She felt the tension spinning in the air and coiling around her, tighter and tighter, strangling as a boa constrictor, while he ruminated. She wished she could see his face and perhaps read a little of what he was thinking from his expression. She wished she could wave a magic wand and see into his heart.

Just when she thought she could bear the suspense no longer, he spoke again. ''Well,'' he said, ''I thought I had everything figured out. Things seemed pretty straightforward, I thought. But they're not, are they? And that puts a whole different slant on things, wouldn't you say? So where do you propose we go from here, Miss *Belles Illusions*?''

CHAPTER TWELVE

"YOU'RE asking me?" she said, puzzled.

"Who else? I'm a man with a child and roots in one place. What have I got to offer that can compete with the kind of high excitement you thrive on?"

"You *want* to compete?" she inquired, sounding as dull-witted as a brick. "But why? Even when you believed I was at least respectable, you didn't think I was the woman for you. Why would you think so now that you know I'm nothing but a mirage sprung from squalor and poverty beyond anything you can begin to imagine?"

"Damned if I know," he said bleakly. "All I can tell you is I'll have a hell of a time watching you walk out of my life."

"You're not making sense, Zachary."

"I know. But then, nothing about what I feel for you has ever made sense."

"Then what has it had to do with, *mon amour*?" she asked, venturing to go to him since he didn't seem disposed to come to her.

"Passion and obsession and sex," he said, his face a study in frustration, "balanced by a burning need to share, to know, to give, to protect. A willingness to change, to become a better man. Hunger so strong that it oozes out of every pore. Emptiness that only you can fill."

He looked haunted, haggard.

"Are you saying you still…love me, after everything I've told you?"

"No," he growled. "I'm saying I don't like pickled cabbage and peanut butter! Of course I'm saying I still love you, for all the good it's doing me!''

"And...?"

"And nothing! I've just laid down my heart for you to trample on, for Pete's sake. Isn't that enough?''

"No," she said, quietly. "I'm afraid it's not."

She waited for him to ask what more she wanted, but he didn't. Instead, he said, "I should have figured it wouldn't be. An international corporate wizard and a stay-at-home father make for a bad—an *impossible* combination. So go back to where you belong, Claire, and put these last days behind you. And while you're doing that, I'll try to take my own advice and forget I ever met you."

And then, he walked out of the door.

The air outside stung his face, bit into his lungs. So, he thought, hunching his shoulders against the cold, that was that. After all the shouting was over and done with, he was exactly where he'd started out with her. Nowhere.

Realistically, it was probably for the best because the only thing they had going was chemistry and that usually burned itself out pretty damn fast. He should be relieved and happy at having proved, conclusively, that it wasn't enough to sustain a relationship over the long haul. But he'd been telling himself that practically from the minute he met her and it hadn't lessened his obsession one iota.

The storm had moved on and left the night full of stars. There was no color anywhere. Black as pallbearers, the trees stood watch beneath mountain tips painted ghostly gray in the faint light. More alone than he'd ever been in his life before, he gazed up at the sky, so high and quiet and indifferent. *Play out your little dramas,* it seemed to say. *They won't impact me.*

"I don't care," he muttered. Why should he? He'd got

all the things that really mattered—the resort, a few good friends, and most of all, Mel.

You hide behind Melanie…without her, you have to face your own needs… Claire had told him once.

He glared at the frost shining like fake diamonds on the surface of the snow and swore with more than usual creative flair. Was he going to have to go through the rest of his life being reminded of her every time he turned around?

Behind him, he heard the hut door open and her footsteps crunch lightly down the steps. She stopped beside him and for a while they did nothing but watch their breaths vaporize in front of their faces.

At last, she said, "I won't settle for being your mistress who lives in Europe and who meets you some place between here and there, where no one will know that we're lovers. I won't do that to myself and I won't do it to Melanie. You have to love me enough to want to marry me."

"Who's talking about marriage?" he growled, stunned.

"I am, because one of us has to and it obviously isn't going to be you."

"You'd better be sure you know what you'd be letting yourself in for," he told her, a flicker of warmth licking through the ice in his veins and melting the cold invading his bones. "*Damn* sure, Claire. Because marrying me means taking on a package deal that would send a lot of women running for the hills.

"I'm not saying I'd expect a woman to give up everything she's worked for but I'd sure as hell want someone who's more wife than business exec cum celebrity socialite. I might not drag my knuckles across the floor when I walk, but I don't pretend to move in the most elite circles either, even if I am on a first-name basis with some who do."

He stopped just long enough to draw breath, knowing

that if he didn't get everything off his chest in one go, he'd be tempted to settle for half measures. But having done that once and paid the price in guilt and regret, he wasn't prepared to do it again. "Not only that, when I'm not on the job, my idea of a good time is stoking up the fire at home and inviting McBride over for barbecued steak. I don't mind a bit of travel once in a while but when it comes to traipsing all over the globe and not belonging anywhere, you can keep it. This is my place in the sun, the place I call home and where I want to spend most of my time."

"Would you like to know what I'm looking for?" she asked, with more than a touch of irony. "Is that of any interest to you at all?"

"I already know. You want to be exactly who you are, living exactly the kind of life you currently enjoy."

"No, Zachary. What I most want has always eluded me and so I settled for the next best thing, which is a life just as you describe it: on the surface very exciting, very rewarding, very comfortable but, *hélas,* with very little below the service."

"Surface," he said.

She shrugged as only she could, with elegant insouciance. "If you prefer. But what I dream about, deep in my heart, is being accepted not for the person people think I am, but for the real me, a woman who would give anything—everything—to love and be loved. To be needed. To be a wife, a mother. To make a home, and wear a plain gold ring which tells the world I belong to one special man.

"You have a few friends and I have many acquaintances, Zachary. Your friends will stay with you regardless of the troubles that might befall you. My acquaintances will disappear the moment ill fortune strikes. I've always known that, which is why I've worked so hard to show a successful face. And for too many years, I've made do with acquaintances because no one came into my life who made me want to reveal my true heart. But now there is you and there is Melanie, and I won't willingly settle for lesser things again.''

She slipped her hand under his elbow and leaned against him. ''As for the travel involved in keeping my businesses alive, a few days a year is all it takes, a week or two at most which could easily be turned into a second honeymoon for us. Rome is not so bad in October and Paris in April is lovely. So, will you let me be your wife, Zachary? Will you let me fill the space in Melanie's life which opened up when she lost her real mother? Will you let me love you and have your babies?''

She might have been born in a slum, but she had the soul and bearing of a queen. She stood there cloaked in quiet dignity, prepared to accept his rejection, to weather his abuse and, more to the point, to survive both. She put him to shame with her courage and generosity.

He opened his mouth to speak, then shut it again, quickly, before the surge of emotion rushing at him with the force of an avalanche bowled him over and made a fool of him. He wanted to bawl like a kid. He wanted to shout to the heavens with elation. He wanted to drop down on his knees and thank God for not giving up on him when he was, most of the time, a perfect ass and ignorant as a boulder.

''How soon do you want to get started?'' he finally managed, daring to look down at her and risk drowning in the fathomless gray pools of her eyes.

She smiled, a Mona Lisa smile hinting at untold pleasures to come, and led him back inside the hut. ''I think we should strike the hot iron,'' she said.

He thought she needed another English lesson, but it

would have to stand in line and take a number. He had a few other things to teach her, first.

Except for the orange hole in the mouth of the stove and a single candle, the interior of the hut snoozed in darkness. With slow reverence, he stripped away her clothes until she stood before him, ethereal in her nakedness, her exquisite, smooth-as-cream skin limned in gold where it was touched with firelight and shadowed with pearl elsewhere.

He took her hand and raised it to his lips. "I can fight the bank, the weather, and even Mel," he said huskily, pressing a kiss to her palm, "but I can't fight you. If you'll have me, Claire, I'm yours for the rest of time."

She swayed toward him, lithe and warm and irresistible. "Then give yourself to me," she whispered and pulling her hand free, began to peel away his clothes. By the time she was done, his pulse was jolting around like a mad thing and he was strung taut as a bow.

He wanted to take things slowly, to savor every inch of her. He started off that way, his fingers tracing idly over her skin, branding her his possession, his treasure. Too briefly, his mouth followed suit, defining the high curve of her breasts, the sweet hollow of her waist, the secret enclave of her femininity.

Quivering beneath his touch, she cried out his name, a soft, urgent plea that lured him to the brink of destruction. Propping himself on his elbows, he cradled her closer. She gazed up at him, her mouth soft and swollen from his kisses, her eyes sultry with desire.

He felt the thrust of her breasts, the slack surrender of her thighs, the delicate moisture that welcomed the intrusion of his flesh. She closed around him, tight and sleek as a second skin, and breathed, "I love you, Zachary."

He would have happily died then, if it hadn't been that he had so much to live for. Desperate to savor every jew-

eled facet of the moment, he focused on the candle and
tried to hold back the tide. But control was beyond him
and the rhythm gained momentum regardless of his efforts
to stop time. "Stay with me," he begged, referring not only
to tomorrow but to right then as he hung on the brink of
oblivion.

"Always," she breathed, and convulsed around him in
a thousand tiny shocks of ecstasy.

The candle flame expanded; grew larger, fiercer, and so
hot, so bright. So *right*. He stared at it, willing himself to
remain in command. But his body had other ideas. It hung
poised in a moment of endless anticipation, then sent the
blood charging through his veins to support the life spilling
from him and flooding into her.

He groaned against her neck, wrapped his arms fiercely
around her, and rode the shudders until, eventually, they
washed him up on the far shores of passion. And he knew
that, for the first time in his life, he held perfection in his
grasp. The miracle was, it would remain with him and il-
luminate the years to come.

The next day, after the greetings and the tears were over
and lunch had been served in her hotel suite, Claire sat back
and watched, an amused and delighted spectator as father
and daughter effected their reconciliation.

"I guess I'm grounded for the next ten years," Melanie
said glumly.

"The next four, certainly," Zachary said, fighting hard
to keep his expression appropriately severe. "Claire and I
have talked it over and we've decided to send you some
place where you'll be supervised twenty-four hours a day
except for when you're let out to visit home."

"Huh?"

"I'm talking about boarding school, Mel. Provided you

still want to go. Of course, Claire and I will miss having you around but I guess we'll just have to learn to live with it.''

"Huh?'' she said again, her gaze swinging suspiciously from her father to the three flutes of champagne he was passing around. "What's he talking about, Claire? And why is he giving me booze to drink when he only ever lets me have a teaspoonful on extra special occasions?''

"This *is* a special occasion, Mel,'' Zachary told her. "You're safe, thank God, despite behaving in a thoroughly foolish and dangerous way, and I've come to realize how lucky I am to have you for a daughter, so I'd like to propose a toast. Here's to a new way of doing things and happier times.'' He raised his own glass and when Melanie followed suit, clinked the rim lightly against hers.

Only then did the import of what he'd said finally sink home. "You're letting me go away to boarding school?'' she squealed. "Really?''

"As soon as it can be arranged. I'm hoping we can set up some interviews while we're in town and get you settled in time for the beginning of the new semester.''

"Oh, goll-ee, Dad, I can hardly wait!''

"Your eagerness to leave the nest is hardly flattering,'' he replied dryly, "but cheers, anyway.''

She still had her nose buried in the glass when he dropped his other bombshell, which was hardly fair of him. "And while we're at it, I'd also like to propose a toast to my future bride and your future stepmother.''

The champagne, Veuve Cliquot and much too good to go to waste, bubbled out of Melanie's mouth even faster than it had gone in. "Bride?'' she choked, and turned enormous, incredulous eyes on Claire. "You mean, Claire? You're going to marry Claire? She's going to stick around and be my new mom? *You're putting me on!*''

"Well," he said, his glance sliding over Claire with such potent intimacy that she felt a blush firing her cheeks, "it's not a done deal until you've put in your two bits' worth which, knowing you, you'll give whether we ask for it or not."

"Like there's anything to say except *do it*, Dad, before she changes her mind!"

Claire knew from the mischief in his eyes when he looked at her a second time that it was all he could do not to reply, "We already *have* done it, and more than once!"

Her body ached pleasurably from the lovemaking they'd shared throughout the previous night and just thinking about it started the sultry rhythm pulsing through her veins all over again. She hadn't thought it possible to experience such joyful fulfillment, or to know such complete certainty that she had, at last, found what she'd searched for for so long.

Still blushing, she looked down before her own eyes betrayed the truth to the sweet innocent beaming at them from across the table.

"We're asking for your blessing, Mel," Zachary said soberly. "That's the only way we'll go through with the wedding."

Melanie snorted impatiently. "Honestly, Dad, sometimes you're so lame! You're not getting any younger, you know, so, like I said, get on with it before she changes her mind. Heck, I thought it was a good idea a long time before it occurred to either of you. The only thing is, you've got to do it before school starts so that I can be at the wedding."

"The sooner, the better, then," Zachary declared. "So let's wrap things up here and go shopping for a diamond." He looked at Claire, the message in his eyes only for her, and his voice was husky with emotion when he added, "It might not be the biggest or the best, but it'll definitely be the real thing, guaranteed to last a lifetime."

HARLEQUIN *Presents*
Passion™

Looking for stories that **sizzle**?

Wanting a read that has a little extra **spice**?

Harlequin Presents® is thrilled to bring you
romances that turn up the **heat!**

Every other month there'll be a
PRESENTS PASSION™
book by one of your favorite authors.

Don't miss
THE SPANISH HUSBAND
by **Michelle Reid**

On sale December, Harlequin Presents® #2145

Pick up a **PRESENTS PASSION**™—
where **seduction** is guaranteed!

Available wherever Harlequin books are sold.

HARLEQUIN®
Makes any time special ™

Visit us at www.eHarlequin.com   HPPASS2

HARLEQUIN®
makes any time special—online...

your romantic
life

➤ Talk to Dr. Romance, find a romantic recipe, or send a virtual hint to the love of your life. You'll find great articles and advice on romantic issues that are close to your heart.

your romantic
books

➤ Visit our *Author's Alcove* and try your hand in the Writing Round Robin—contribute a chapter to an online book in the making.

➤ Enter the *Reading Room* for an interactive novel—help determine the fate of a story being created now by one of your favorite authors.

➤ Drop into *Shop eHarlequin* to buy the latest releases—read an excerpt, find this month's Harlequin top sellers.

your romantic
escapes

➤ Escape into romantic movies at *Reel Love*, learn what the stars have in store for you with *Lovescopes*, treat yourself to our *Indulgences Guides* and get away to the latest romantic hot spots in *Romantic Travel*.

All this and more available at
www.eHarlequin.com
on Women.com Networks

HECHAN1R

ROMANTIC FANTASIES COME ALIVE WITH

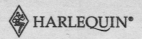

HARLEQUIN®

INTIMACIES

Harlequin is turning up the heat with this seductive collection!

Experience the passion as the heroes and heroines explore their deepest desires, their innermost secrets. Get lost in these tantalizing stories that will leave you wanting more!

Available in November at your favorite retail outlet:

OUT OF CONTROL by Candace Schuler
NIGHT RHYTHMS by Elda Minger
SCANDALIZED! by Lori Foster
PRIVATE FANTASIES by Janelle Denison

Visit us at www.eHarlequin.com   PHINT1

This Christmas, experience the love, warmth and magic that only Harlequin can provide with

Mistletoe Magic

a charming collection from

BETTY NEELS
MARGARET WAY   REBECCA WINTERS

Available November 2000

HARLEQUIN®
Makes any time special ™

Visit us at www.eHarlequin.com

PHMAGIC

CELEBRATE VALENTINE'S DAY WITH HARLEQUIN®'S LATEST TITLE—

Stolen Memories

Available in trade-size format, this collector's edition contains three full-length novels by *New York Times* bestselling authors Jayne Ann Krentz and Tess Gerritsen, along with national bestselling author Stella Cameron.

TEST OF TIME by **Jayne Ann Krentz**—
He married for the best reason.... She married for the only reason.... Did they stand a chance at making the only reason the real reason to share a lifetime?

THIEF OF HEARTS by **Tess Gerritsen**—
Their distrust of each other was only as strong as their desire. And Jordan began to fear that Diana was more than just a thief of hearts.

MOONTIDE by **Stella Cameron**—
For Andrew, Greer's return is a miracle. It had broken his heart to let her go. Now fate has brought them back together. And he won't lose her again...

Make this Valentine's Day one to remember!

Look for this exciting collector's edition on sale January 2001 at your favorite retail outlet.

HARLEQUIN®
Makes any time special ™

Visit us at www.eHarlequin.com

PHSM